GHOST LIES

Love & Lies Book 3

Alex Strong

Red Dahlia Publishing

Ghost Lies

Cover Art © Aarrttuurr/BortN66/fotolia
Cover Design by J.P. Irons

ISBN: 978-0-9964709-1-9

For everyone who believed in me. Especially my dad.

One

Agent Gavin Maxwell was leaning against the wall checking emails on his phone when Director Laura Rollins walked into the small observation room.

"They're bringing her in now," she said.

Seconds later, a door opened on the other side of the one-way glass and a tall blonde woman walked in, followed by a male police officer who directed her to the seat facing the one-way glass.

"So this is Tristan Brandt's fiancée," Gavin muttered.

"Was," Rollins corrected.

Gavin studied Sydney Holden while Officer Desmond made sure the recording equipment was working.

She looked as he would expect a woman in mourning to look—dressed in jeans and flats, a tan sweater wrapped around her. Her hair was pulled into a bun with loose tresses escaping, the longest of which framed her face. Her blue eyes were puffy from what Gavin guessed was crying or lack of sleep. Most likely both.

"Thank you, Miss Holden, for coming in to talk to us," said Officer Desmond, now ready to ask the questions provided to him by Director Rollins.

Sydney nodded, and Gavin noticed she was massaging something in her right hand. Squinting, he leaned closer against the glass and realized it was a wadded tissue.

"She looks genuinely distraught," he said.

"I'm sure Bonnie would have been just as distraught had she survived Clyde," said Rollins.

Sydney spoke for the first time since entering the interrogation room. "I still don't understand why you need to talk to me."

"We just have a few questions about your fiancé that we were hoping you could answer for us."

"Um, okay." But it was clear she was still confused. Gavin wondered if it was all an act.

"First off," Desmond started, "what can you tell us about what Mr. Brandt did for a living?"

"He's an art dealer. Was," she corrected with a sniff. "He owned a gallery in Pioneer Square. But you guys know that, don't you?"

"Was he involved in anything else beyond that?" he asked, ignoring her question.

"Well, sure," she said. "He sat on a few boards. Some non-profit organizations, mostly arts-related. What is this all about?" she asked, more demanding this time.

"Were you aware that he was involved in any illegal activities?"

"That he was what?" Her eyes nearly popped out of her head. "That's ridiculous!" she said, shaking her head.

Gavin watched Desmond pull a picture from a folder and slide it towards Sydney.

"Do you know who this is?" Desmond asked.

She pulled the picture closer. "This is Aleksandr Morozov. He is—was a client of Tristan's."

"Aleksandr Morozov," Desmond said, taking the picture back, "was the head of a crime syndicate."

"He was...." She trailed off and cocked her head. Gavin could see the wheels turning, as though she were piecing things together. Behavior, comments perhaps.

"What does that have to do with Tristan?" she finally asked. "There's no way he was involved with anything illegal."

"Is that your story?" asked Desmond.

"My story? What the hell is this about? You can't honestly think—"

"We know for a fact that your fiancé was doing more than just buying art from Mr. Morozov. The question is whether or not you were involved in any of it."

Sydney stood up, and Gavin could see her sadness being replaced by anger.

"I think we're done here," she said. "How dare you suggest that Tristan or I—"

She stopped talking when Desmond slapped two more photos on the table and Sydney looked like she was going to be sick.

"Are those the container pictures?" Gavin asked Rollins, who nodded.

"This is a shipping container that was supposed to be claimed by your fiancé."

Sydney dropped back down into her chair, shaking her head again.

"It was full of young women. The first picture is the women who were still alive by the time anyone got to it. The second is the ones who weren't."

"There's no way," said Sydney. "How can you possibly think that this has anything to do with Tristan?"

"The customs agent that was working for Mr. Brandt came forward after the container went uncollected. Apparently his guilt finally got the best of him."

Gavin watched as Sydney closed her eyes and buried her face in her hands; he saw her shoulders shake, but no sound came from her.

"She didn't know," he said.

"Agreed," said Rollins.

***

Six Months Later

"What's this?" Gavin Maxwell asked, opening the file that Director Laura Rollins had placed on his desk. "Sydney Holden? I thought this case was closed."

"Recent intel suggests that Tristan Brandt may still be alive."

"Just as Casimir warned," Gavin sighed.

"I need you to get close to his former girlfriend."

"But I thought we questioned her and decided that she didn't know anything. Even Casimir said he didn't think she was working with him."

"He could have been wrong," said Rollins. "And maybe she's just as good at lying as he was. Truth is they were living together, so it stands to reason that if he faked his death, she would know something. Maybe it was all part of the plan. He pretends to die, she pretends to mourn."

Gavin scanned the dossier. His eyes stopped at a possible lead.

"I may know a way to approach her," he said.

***

Sydney focused on the hold above her head. It was only six inches from her hand, but it may as well have been ten feet. She took a deep breath and pushed off with her leg, but the second her right hand reached for it, the left arm gave out—again—and down she fell to the thick mat below. Her feet hit first and she willingly let the rest of her body fall back. A groan escaped Sydney as she looked up at the route on the climbing wall she had been tackling all morning, only to be defeated again and again.

She sat up and looked at the clock over the front desk before moving over to the bench. She started to pull a shoe off when someone sat down next to her. Out of the corner of her eye, she could tell it was the same tall, dark stranger she had noticed earlier.

"You aren't giving up yet, are you?" he asked.

She laughed as she pulled off the other shoe. "No, but I think my arms are."

"I think you're using the wrong foot on the purple hold." She looked up and saw where he was pointing to a spot along the route. "You put your right foot on it. I know it's a little awkward, but if you put your left foot on, it would give you the leverage to push up to the last one."

Like any experienced climber, Sydney's hands started mimicking the movements. "You might be right," she said. Another glance at the clock told her she was running out of time. If she braided her hair instead of blow drying it, she could still make it to her meeting on time.

Sydney slipped her climbing shoes back on, dug into the chalk bag one last time, and approached the wall with the handsome stranger following her. She got to the purple hold he had indicated and wanted badly to place her right foot on it, but this time she stepped on a lower hold that she had been skipping and awkwardly placed her left foot on the purple one. And when she went for the last hold at the top, it was exactly what she needed. From this point, Sydney climbed over the top of the wall and walked along the ledge to the ladder.

"Thank you," she said with a big grin to her new companion when she was back down on the floor. "I can't believe I didn't think of that."

"I'm sure you would've gotten there on your own," he said with a shrug. "I'm Gavin, by the way." He held out a hand and Sydney took it.

"Sydney Holden," she said, watching for a flicker of recognition at her name. It'd been in so many headlines not that long ago, after all. When it was clear the name meant nothing to him, she sat down and peeled off her shoes again.

Gavin pulled his bag out from one of the cubbies and dug out a pair of regular shoes.

"I was going to go grab coffee across the street. Care to join me?" he asked.

Sydney smiled, wondering if this had been his plan all along. "Unfortunately I'm going to have to book it if I'm going to make it to work," she said. "But maybe next time."

His face broke into a rugged grin. "Maybe next

time."

Sydney picked up her bag and walked out feeling flattered by the attention. She wondered if he was new to the area.

***

It was hard to keep the smile off Sydney's face when she walked into the climbing gym a week later and spotted Gavin halfway up a wall. He was using a rope this time, which meant he got to climb higher, but she recognized one of the gym's employees belaying from the ground.

Feeling bold, she walked over and watched as he reached the top of a difficult route before pushing off the wall and letting his belay buddy lower him back to the earth.

"Hello again," he said when he caught sight of her.

"Hello," she answered.

"Care to take a try?" he asked.

"Afraid I left my harness at home," she said. "Maybe next time."

"Maybe next time," he said with a sexy smile that made his hazel eyes light up.

"Thanks again for helping me get past that last

route."

"My pleasure. I see they've changed the routes since then. Good thing you conquered it last week."

"Then I guess I'll have to go find a new challenge."

"Let me know if you need any help," he said.

She laughed as she walked over to the bouldering section. "Will do."

An hour later and Sydney's arms were about to give out. But from the corner of her eye she could see Gavin, who had moved over to the bouldering section as well, still going strong. She wondered if he had the same stamina in bed but quickly shook her head, surprised by the thought. It had been so long since her thoughts had strayed in that direction. Not since Tristan....

Sydney moved over to the bench and prepared to head home. It had been a long day.

Gavin appeared at her side not long after.

"I realize it's kind of late for coffee, but I hear there's a pub not far from here that has good beer and wouldn't judge us if we showed up in our sweaty workout clothes."

She focused on something in the distance, contemplating his suggestion. After the day she'd had, she could certainly use a drink. And as much as she hated to admit it, her mother was right; it was time for her to get back out there.

"I could use a beer," she said.

His face lit up. "Great." He gave her the address and got up to leave. "See you in a few."

***

From a table in the middle of the bar, Gavin waved Sydney over when she walked in only moments after he had snagged the table. He would have preferred one of the private booths, but he needed Sydney to feel safe, and being out on the open floor would be more likely to help her feel so.

"You made it," he said as she sat on the bar stool.

"Thank you for inviting me," she said. "This is exactly what I needed."

A server appeared and took their orders.

"Rough day?" Gavin asked when they were left alone.

"You can say that again," she said.

"What do you do?" he asked, as if he didn't already know.

"I'm in charge of security protocol for a major bank

in Seattle."

"That sounds like something that could be stressful."

"It certainly has its days. It doesn't help that I'm on-call twenty-four seven. If there's a problem with any of the systems, I'm the one they call to make sure all proper procedures are followed."

Their beers were set on the table, and Sydney took a long drink from her glass before continuing.

"What about you?" she asked. "What do you do?"

This was where Gavin would normally answer with the standard cover of working in banking security, but given Sydney's similar background, he fell back to one of his other aliases.

"I'm a computer programmer," he told her.

"A computer geek," she said. "Do you work for Microsoft?"

"I freelance."

"That must be nice, being your own boss and everything."

"It has its advantages," he said with a smile.

"Is that why I see you at the gym at different times of the day?"

So she had noticed him other than just the day he approached her. So far so good.

"My schedule's flexible," he said. "It seems yours is as well."

"Sometimes," she said.

The chit chat continued, and when they were about halfway through a second round, Gavin knew it was time to make the next move.

"You should have dinner with me tomorrow night," he said casually.

Sydney's glass stopped halfway to her mouth. She set it down and cleared her throat.

"Dinner?" she asked.

Gavin leaned across the table and stared right into her bright blue eyes. They were quite beautiful. "Yes, dinner."

"Tomorrow night?"

He nodded. "Do you have plans?"

"No," she said, shaking her head. "Dinner sounds nice. What did you have in mind?"

Gavin looked up at the ceiling, pretending to think about it.

"How about eight o'clock at Icon Grill? Do you

know where that is?"

"I'm familiar with it."

"Do you want me to pick you up?" he asked.

"I can meet you there," she said. "It's not far from where I live."

"Perfect." Gavin finished off his beer and stood. "I'll see you tomorrow night."

"Great," she said, giving him an excited smile.

This was going exactly as planned.

***

Sydney stood outside the door to the Icon Grill, hesitating. All day she had gone back and forth about canceling. In fact, the only reason she was here was because she had no way to contact Gavin and wouldn't have been able to face him at the gym again if she stood him up. *It's just dinner,* she tried to remind herself.

Someone walked out and she could see Gavin standing near the hostess both. His face lit up at the sight of her, and she couldn't help but smile back.

What could be the harm in having dinner with a nice guy? An *attractive,* nice guy.

"Hi," she said when she was standing next to him.

"How was your day?" he asked. "Better than

yesterday, I hope?"

"Much."

The hostess grabbed two menus and led them beneath the hand-blown glass chandeliers to a small booth against a wall covered in an eclectic collection of local art.

"Your server should be with you shortly," she said and disappeared.

"Have you eaten here before?" Sydney asked.

"Once. It was years ago though. You?"

"I used to come for brunch. They have great mimosas."

"Used to?" he asked with a frown.

Sydney looked around at the familiar decor. It was strange that she had not remembered all those Sunday mornings with Tristan until now. But then she had been doing her best to not think about him for the past six months.

She shook her head and gave a shrug. "Habits change. Not much of a brunch person anymore." Sydney was determined to enjoy this evening with Gavin.

A gentleman appeared to tell them about the specials and take their drink orders.

"How long have you lived in Seattle?" Sydney

asked when they were alone again.

"I lived here years ago, but until two months ago, I was living down in California."

Sydney wondered if this was why he hadn't recognized her name. But then she reminded herself that there were plenty of people who didn't know who she was or her connection to Tristan Brandt.

"How about yourself?" Gavin asked. "Where did you grow up?"

"Well, I've always lived in Washington," she said, "but I grew up on the other side of the state near Spokane. I came out here for college and never left."

"How did you end up in banking security?"

"I stumbled into it. During college I worked as a teller and eventually found myself in this position. It wasn't what I planned to do, but now I love it. Turns out I enjoy being the go-to person, the crisis solver. When something goes wrong, I'm the one they call to fix it."

"Sounds exciting," said Gavin, who had never broken eye contact with her the whole time she had been speaking. Sydney was impressed she'd been able to keep her train of thought with those hazel eyes staring into her own.

"What about you?" she asked. "Did you always want to be a computer programmer?"

He leaned back and rested an arm across the top of the plush booth. "I did. Even as a kid I was always tinkering on the computer. Developed my first game at the age of thirteen."

"Wow, now that's impressive."

Gavin gave a modest smile. "I'm just happy that something I enjoyed doing as a kid is paying the bills."

The server reappeared with their glasses of wine and took their meal orders.

"Can I propose a toast?" Gavin asked, raising his glass.

She nodded and lifted hers.

"Here's to loving what we do. And to making new friends."

"Cheers," Sydney said, smiling.

They clinked glasses and she was just taking her first sip when Sydney heard the all-too-familiar ring tone.

"I'm so sorry," she said, setting down her glass. "I'm afraid that would be the bank."

"Of course," he said.

She pulled the phone from her bag and was halfway

to the waiting area before she answered it, praying it would be a simple fix.

"Sydney Holden," she said.

"Sydney, it's Jerry. There's been a break-in attempt."

Two

Gavin gave himself a mental pat on the back while waiting for Sydney to return. Everything was going well. He was even enjoying himself. But then he caught the look on Sydney's face as she made her way back to the table.

"Is everything all right?" he asked, standing as she approached.

"I have to go," she said, rummaging through her bag. "I can't tell you how sorry I am." She pulled out her wallet and unzipped it.

"Don't worry, I've got this," he said, realizing what she was trying to do.

"No, I insist." She tossed down a couple bills on the table before he could stop her. "You invited me out and now I have to leave before the first course even arrives."

"What happened?" he asked, gently placing a hand on her arm. "You're clearly frazzled."

She looked around and then leaned in close to him. "There's been a break-in attempt. I have to go and make sure everyone does everything by the book. Make sure it was only an attempt."

"Do you need me to give you a ride?"

"I'll catch a cab, it's fine. You should stay and enjoy our dinners. Or at least get them to go so someone can enjoy them." And she rushed off before he could say anything else.

Gavin watched her walk out the door before sinking back into the booth. The server must have witnessed the scene, because she arrived only moments later asking if there was a problem.

"I'm afraid my date had an emergency. Could I get those meals boxed up please?" he said.

"Of course."

"And the check as well," he called after her.

Gavin realized they still hadn't exchanged contact info, which meant he was going to have to spend more time at the gym again. Not that he didn't already have all her phone numbers and her address, but that would spook her. Besides, he looked forward to seeing her in her climbing shorts again.

***

The yellow taxi dropped Sydney off in front of the bank and a uniformed police officer verified her ID before letting her in.

Her high heels echoed throughout the marbled lobby as she crossed to where Jerry was standing with Saul, the night security guard, another uniformed officer, and two suited gentlemen.

"Ah," said Jerry, "here she is."

One of the suits offered his hand as she approached.

"You must be Sydney Holden," he said.

She nodded and took his hand.

"I'm Detective Gund, and this is Detective Miller," he said, and the other gentleman shook her hand as well.

"I've explained to these gentleman that you're here just to make sure proper procedure is followed," said Jerry.

"Shall we get started then?" asked Gund.

To Sydney's surprise, they headed in the direction of the security deposit boxes rather than the vault. She listened as Jerry told the officers what had happened.

"We still don't know how the guy got past our security systems, but once he was in, he sneaked up on the first guard and incapacitated him before going to work on the gate."

There were marks on one of the metal bars where someone had attempted to cut through. By the black residue, Sydney guessed a small torch or laser cutting tool.

"When Saul arrived for his shift, he heard the noise," Jerry continued, "and called it in before trying to apprehend the person. Unfortunately, Saul was overtaken and the would-be thief got away."

"Miller," said Gund, "you take Saul aside and get a proper statement from him and any description he can provide."

Miller nodded and moved with Saul to one of the counters.

"What happened to the other guard?" Sydney asked.

"He's at the hospital," said Jerry. "He was injected with something, but I haven't heard back from anyone at the hospital yet."

"We have an officer there now," said Gund. He made some notes on his pad then looked up again. "He knew to take out the first guard but not the second. Have you always had two night guards?"

"There was only one until a month or so ago," Jerry answered.

"Why is that?" asked Gund.

"I proposed it to the board," said Sydney. "Previously we had one man working a twelve-hour shift; I thought it would be more effective to have two overlapping ten-hour shifts."

"Interesting," Gund said, scratching on his pad again. "So it's possible our perp was working with old information."

"But where would he get that information?" Sydney asked. "Most of our employees don't even know the logistics of our overnight security."

"You'd be surprised, Miss Holden. Now let's talk about the boxes."

Gund turned to peer through the gate and Sydney stood next to him with Jerry on the other side of her. Her next breath caught a whiff of something familiar, but why would she smell it now, here of all places? She inhaled deeper and it was gone. Had she really smelled it?

"In my experience," Gund said, cutting into her thoughts, "when people go after the boxes and not the vault, they're after something specific. It's too much of a gamble to go after them blind." He turned to Sydney and Jerry. "Any idea what our guy may have been after?"

"You know we have no idea what's in any of them," said Jerry.

"I figured as much," said Gund. "But sometimes people hear rumors. You never know."

Jerry shook his head. "Sorry."

"Walk me through security now," Gund said, and Sydney followed them as Jerry explained all the security measures that had been successfully bypassed. At the moment, Sydney was glad she wasn't the person in charge of security, only in enforcing it. Jerry was going to have some explaining to do.

When the police had done all that they could, Jerry was handed a copy of the police report to give to insurance for replacing the now-compromised gate.

As Sydney crawled into bed just before two in the morning, exhausted beyond belief, her thoughts drifted back to the break-in and the cologne she thought she had detected. It had to have been her imagination, but why would she have dreamt of Tristan? Because of her date with Gavin, perhaps? Now that thought brought a smile to her face. Sydney realized that in her rush she had forgotten to give him her phone number, but she had a feeling it wouldn't be the last time she'd see him. And she was looking forward to it.

***

When Sydney walked into the gym Monday morning, she was delighted to find Gavin at a bench. He was packing up his stuff, but at least she could apologize again.

He looked up before she made it to him, and her heart skipped a beat at his obvious pleasure in seeing her.

"Well hello there," he said.

"Are you heading out?" she asked, gesturing to his bag.

"Afraid so."

"I still feel horrible about Friday night," she said.

"Don't worry about it. You warned me that you had a twenty-four hour job."

"I don't normally have to run off like that. Most problems I can walk people through."

Gavin slung the bag over his shoulder. "It happens."

"I was hoping that I could make it up to you, though."

A small smile appeared on his face, and Sydney felt her pulse quicken.

"What did you have in mind?" he asked.

"How about dinner at my place? Tomorrow night?"

"Are you offering to cook for me?" he asked.

"Yes, I am," she said, blushing. "I happen to be an excellent cook."

He took a step closer to her, and Sydney resisted the desire to reach out and touch his solid chest. She could only imagine how it might feel against her skin.

"Then I'd be crazy to say no," he said. "Do you have a pen?"

Sydney forced herself to look away so that she could dig a pen out of her bag. When she handed it to him, he grabbed her hand and wrote a number on her forearm.

"Text me your address and a good time to come over."

"Okay," she whispered.

"See you tomorrow."

Her arm tingled where he had touched her, and she wondered if that was why Gavin had written it for her instead of just keying it directly into their phones. As he walked out of the gym, Sydney wished she had invited him over for that night instead of tomorrow.

**

Gavin arrived at Sydney's building with five minutes to spare. He checked the eavesdropping devices in his jacket pocket before grabbing the flowers and wine bottle from the back seat.

When Sydney greeted him at the door with a big, beautiful smile, Gavin had to remind himself, not for the first time, that this was an operation. Sydney Holden was a possible source of information. And the fact that she was looking incredible in a tank top that showed off her perfectly-sculpted arms did nothing to change that.

"Are those for me?" she asked, breaking his train of thought.

"Of course," he said, looking at the gifts in his hand. "I was taught to never show up empty-handed."

"Thank you," she said, taking the flowers and wine from him. "Come in."

As Sydney walked in front of him, Gavin saw a bare foot peek out with each step beneath her full-length cotton skirt and found it irresistibly sexy.

In the kitchen, she placed the flowers in a vase and set his pinot noir next to an already open bottle of Cabernet

Sauvignon.

"I rarely cook without a glass in hand," she explained, pouring him a glass.

"Something smells amazing," he said, taking the glass from her.

"That would be the salmon roasting in the oven."

"And what's in here?" he asked, looking into a pan on the stove. "Is this risotto?"

She nodded.

"I'm impressed already," he said.

"Best to save the compliments until after you've actually tasted it," she said, sliding in next to him to add more stock to the rice dish. "It's almost done, though, if you want to make yourself at home."

Gavin knew this was his chance.

"Where should I put my jacket?" he asked.

"There's a coat closet by the door, but feel free to toss it on one of the chairs in the living room."

Still holding his glass of wine, Gavin moved out to the other room and pulled a couple "bugs" out of his pocket. He set the glass down, removed his coat, and placed the listening device under one of her end tables. Looking around, he saw a console table in the front hall with some framed pictures. He moved closer and found a photo of Sydney and another woman who had to be her sister or at least a close relative. He pressed another device to the back of it.

"Is this your sister?" he asked, picking up the picture.

Sydney poked her head out.

"My cousin. But everyone confuses us as sisters."

"Do you have any siblings?"

"Just a brother. He lives in Colorado."

Gavin walked up to the dining table that was in view of the kitchen where Sydney had her back to him, so he quickly reached underneath and attached another device. Now the only part of the condo he didn't have ears on was her bedroom, but he wasn't sure how to get in there yet.

"What about your family?" Sydney asked as she pulled the salmon out. "Do you have any siblings?"

"Only child," he said.

"And where did you say your parents lived?"

"I didn't."

Sydney turned to look at him and Gavin waited for her to say something else, but she must have realized he didn't want to talk about it.

"Dinner's ready," she said with a smile.

***

Gavin refilled the wine glasses with the bottle he'd brought while Sydney took away the dirty dishes and grabbed dessert.

"I'm not sure I could eat another bite," he said as she set a ramekin of tiramisu in front of him.

"Well then I will gladly eat it for you," she said, reaching for his dish.

He grabbed her wrist and saw her flush at his touch.

"I didn't say I wasn't going to try," he said, giving her a sly smile.

She made no attempt to pull her arm from his grip, and he eventually let go. There was a hint of a something playful in her eyes as she looked down at her own dish and dug in. Sydney was not making this easy for him. It was time to get down to business.

"You weren't lying," he said after taking a bite of the rich espresso dessert. "You do know how to make a great meal."

"Thank you," she said.

Gavin took another spoonful, trying to come up with the right words.

"So I told a buddy that I was going out tonight," he said slowly, "and I happened to mention your name."

Her whole body went rigid, and Gavin was sad to see the relaxed air disappear.

"And let me guess," she said. "He'd heard of me before."

"You're not surprised?"

Sydney pushed her half-eaten dessert back and reached for her glass of wine.

"I suppose it was bound to come out eventually," she said.

"Were you really involved with an arms dealer?" he asked as though he hadn't pored over all the transcripts of her questioning.

She took a huge drink of wine before answering his question.

"For the record, I didn't know what he really was." She stared at the red liquid in her glass. "Even when it all came to light, I refused to believe it. I was sure they had him confused with someone else."

"But how did you not know?" Gavin asked without thinking.

Sydney stood, taking her dish and wine glass over

to the kitchen. Gavin jumped up and followed her.

"I'm sorry," he said, coming up behind her. "I had no right to ask that."

She turned to face him with a hard look in her eyes. "Don't you think I ask myself that all the time? Do you know how naive, how *stupid* I felt? When he died, I was devastated. I was a fucking mess. And then to find out that the man I was mourning never even really existed. It was all a lie."

Gavin touched her cheek and she closed her eyes. Her face began to soften again, and it was all he could do not to kiss her right now.

"I told myself," she said, opening her eyes, "that I would never be able to trust anyone again." Gavin could barely hear her next words. "That I would never let anyone get this close to me."

As she stood there staring at him, Gavin traced a line down to her throat where he could feel her pulse quickening. Or was that his own heartbeat? Without thinking about it, his lips parted, waiting to see what would happen next.

It must have been the invitation she was waiting for, because next thing he knew, Sydney was pressing her lips against his mouth; while the rational part of his brain said it was time to leave, the rest of his body was screaming this was exactly where he wanted to be.

"All I ask," she said, taking a step back and looking him right in the eye, "is that you're honest with me."

Gavin's heart sank, knowing he had already betrayed her. But rather than lie yet again, he kissed her even harder, and it seemed to be the answer she was looking for as she wrapped her arms around his neck and threaded her fingers through his hair. He gripped her hips, pulling her harder into him, and she tugged at his hair. Not hard, just enough to push him closer to the edge. There was no way he was walking away now. He began balling up the skirt until he had room to wrap her legs around him as he lifted her off the floor.

"Where's your bedroom?" he growled into the kiss.

She giggled as she tugged his bottom lip with her teeth. "That way," she said, nodding to his left.

***

As Gavin carried her the short distance to her bedroom, Sydney felt the butterflies beat harder against her stomach. For days she had been wondering how his skin would feel against hers, craving it even after yesterday, and here she was getting her wish.

They made it only two steps into the room before he was pressing her against the wall and he let a leg drop, moving the free hand between her head and the wall. While his lips worked their way down her neck, her fingers made quick work of the buttons on his shirt. She dug her short nails into his smooth, hard chest and he responded by returning to her mouth and kissing her with a ferocity, a hunger. There was a lingering taste of wine on his tongue, and it was just as intoxicating as the drink.

She felt the hand still holding her leg around him slide up the back of her thigh and cup her bare ass cheek thanks to the thong she was wearing. A single finger hooked the thin piece of fabric and she shuddered, but he tortured her by removing his hand altogether and releasing the leg so that he could push up on her tank top.

"Your skin feels like it's on fire," he muttered into her neck.

"I'm pretty sure it is right now," she said breathlessly.

"We should do something about that."

"Oh, God, please," she whimpered.

Using both hands, Gavin pulled her tank top off

over her head and removed her bra. But the skin beneath his open shirt was just as hot, and as he pressed his chest against her, she thought she would burst into flames. She pushed him away, and as he pulled his shirt off, she pushed down her skirt and underwear. All that was left now were his jeans. Sydney continued to push him back towards the bed as he undid the belt and zipper, but he fell back onto the bed with a chuckle before either had a chance to pull them down. She climbed upon his seated figure, placing a knee on either side of him, and wrapped her arms around his neck.

"You're completely naked," he said as ran his hands up her back, sending shivers to the very ends of her fingers and toes.

"Yes, I am," she said, giving him a mischievous smile.

"You're beautiful."

She looked into his eyes. His face, his words—they were so sincere. And they were causing the room to spin around her, as though she were falling. She kissed him, and Gavin let them both fall backwards onto the bed so that now she was laying on top of him. He pulled her ponytail holder out and she felt her hair slide across her shoulders and down over her face. She sat up, and together they pushed his jeans down until he was able to kick them off onto the floor. She was about to climb onto him when he rolled her onto her back.

"What's the rush?" he said, his fingers gently caressing the space between her breasts. But they didn't stop there. As they moved down her torso, his lips left a trail of kisses in their wake. And when his hand was reaching between her legs, her hips lifted ever so slightly off the bed. Soon his mouth found its way and the hand pushed a leg to the side. Sydney moaned in anticipation as her hips rose even higher to meet him. Euphoria swept over her as he worked her with his tongue, and she found herself caught between wanting the sensation to last forever and wanting to lose control already. But Gavin made the choice for her when he paused and worked his way back up her chest, pausing at each breast. Beneath him, her legs were writhing in need, wrapping around him and desperately trying to bring his pelvis closer to her. He hovered just above her with a taunting smile. Deciding she'd had enough of his teasing, Sydney wrestled Gavin onto his back and straddled him.

"You're stronger than you look," he said.

She leaned forward to kiss him, slowly grinding against his hips. "I don't like to be kept waiting," she said.

"Duly noted," he grinned.

Sydney was right—he had the same stamina in bed as he did at the rock gym. Every time she thought she had nothing left, he succeeded in arousing just one more orgasm from her until she finally collapsed on the bed next to him.

"You're not done already, are you?" he asked, running a finger along the curvature of her breast. The touch alone was almost enough to set her off.

She was breathing so hard she could barely respond. "I think I might explode."

"What if I go slow?" he asked as he carefully slid back into her.

She fought the urge to push him off as her body started to convulse immediately, but she welcomed the feeling of him in her, of his body this close to hers. And he kept his promise of going slower, gentler, until the very end, when she could feel his body tensing up. His thrusts became quicker and she tried to keep up, but just as he finally climaxed, one last orgasm was torn from her. It was so intense, she bit down on the closest thing, Gavin's shoulder, and heard him cry out, something primal that made her want to bite down even more, but she refrained.

Now it was Gavin's turn to collapse next to her, breathless. Sydney found the strength to roll over and kiss the bite mark on his left shoulder.

"Do you do that often?" he asked, facing her.

"I am so sorry," she muttered into his arm. "I have never done that before. I don't know what came over me."

He grinned and she knew that it was him. He was what came over her. Gavin pulled her head closer and kissed her.

"Can't say I minded it much," he said.

She blushed, but smiled as she rested her head on his chest and listened to the beating of his heart. Even at a quickened pace it was so strong and steady, just like the rest of him.

***

Gavin ran a hand through Sydney's hair, thinking about the line he had just crossed. It was so wrong. So, so wrong. He never intended to take it this far. Why was this so different? Why hadn't he been able to control himself?

Sydney jumped up, interrupting his attempt at remorse.

"Be right back," she said as she bounced out of the room completely naked.

Noise could be heard in the kitchen and Gavin sat up, using pillows to prop himself against the headboard. Now would be a really good time to say goodnight, he told himself. But when she walked back into the room carrying a ramekin and spoon, he was no closer to leaving than he had been a half hour ago.

"What is that?" he asked as she climbed onto the bed and kneeled, facing him.

She spooned some of the tiramisu into her mouth. "I was hungry and remembered I still had half my dessert left."

He laughed and leaned forward. "Are you going to share with me?"

"I only brought one spoon," she said, and took another bite.

"You just let me explore every inch of your body with my tongue," he said, "and now you aren't willing to share a spoon with me."

She didn't say anything as she took another spoonful, a big one, and slowly moved it towards her sensuous mouth, but he caught her wrist with his hand and saw the playfulness again in her eyes. There was no struggle as he brought the hand closer to his face and licked the creamy dessert off the spoon. He watched with pleasure as a small quiver swept through her.

"Why don't you want to talk about your parents?" she asked, scraping out the last little bit in the dish. She offered it to him, but he shook his head and leaned back against the bed.

"There isn't much to say," he said.

"Are they…still around?"

"Why are you so curious?" he asked and she shrugged.

"Just trying to get to know you. You seemed to shut me down when I brought it up earlier," she said, placing the empty dish on the nightstand.

"And now that you have me in your bed, you thought I might open up?"

She pulled her knees up and wrapped her arms around them. "You don't have to if you don't want to, of course. I'm just cautious around people with secrets."

Now Gavin understood. He leaned forward and tucked her hair behind an ear.

"I never knew my dad," he said, "and my mom lost

all custody of me by the time I was ten. Spent the next eight years in the foster care system."

"God, that's awful!"

"It wasn't that bad. I lucked out, ended up in some decent homes, discovered computers, and managed to make the best of my situation. I learned to be very adaptable."

"Then why are you so reluctant to talk about it?" she asked.

"As I said, there isn't much to say, and people tend to feel sorry for me when they know. I don't need their sympathy, so I choose not to bring it up."

"It doesn't make me feel sorry for you," she said, scooting closer to him.

"No?" he said with a smile.

"No, it makes me admire you that much more."

Gavin cupped her face and pulled her mouth to his. He was in so much trouble.

***

Daylight was still a couple hours away when Gavin slid out of bed, leaving a peaceful Sydney snuggled under the covers. He tiptoed out to the kitchen to break a bud from the bouquet and left it on her bedside table. He realized how cliché it was, but he still wanted to leave some gesture that last night meant something to him. He knew their time together was limited, no matter how much he wished things could be different.

***

Showered and shaved, Gavin walked into the agency later that morning and headed straight for Director Rollins' office.

"Good morning, Agent Maxwell," she said from behind her desk as he closed the door behind him. "How did things go last night?"

"She doesn't know anything," he said, sitting on the arm of a couch in her office. It was no secret that the director had spent many a nights on this piece of furniture during some of the more stressful times. "If Brandt is still alive, she's just as clueless as the rest of us."

"And you're absolutely sure?" she asked with narrowed eyes.

"Yes," he said. "I'm sure you've heard the tapes by now."

"I did," she said, standing up. She moved to the front of her desk and leaned against it with her arms crossed. "And I agree with your assessment."

Gavin started to stand, but Rollins wasn't finished

yet.

"It is also my assessment, based on the recordings, that you have gotten too close to Miss Holden."

Gavin resisted the urge to hang his head in shame. It would only make things worse.

"Now that we know she is of no value to us," Rollins continued, "this operation is terminated. You are to go in, recover the listening devices, and explain to Miss Holden that you will no longer be able to see her. That is to be your final contact."

Gavin nodded.

"Is that understood?" Rollins barked, looking for verbal confirmation.

"Yes, Director Rollins, I understand."

"Good. Dismissed."

***

Sydney walked through the door and thought she was imagining the smell of spices and music coming from the kitchen. But the Vivaldi echoing down the hall was no dream, nor the vase of fresh white roses on the coffee table. Just like the ones Tristan brought her whenever he returned from a business trip.

She heard noise in the kitchen, something other than

the music, and she slowly made her way in that direction, wondering who was playing this cruel, sick joke on her. But who else possibly knew about the roses and Tristan's affinity for Vivaldi?

Sydney stepped into the kitchen and came face to face with a ghost.

"Hello, Love. Did you miss me?"

Three

The room started to spin, and Sydney gripped the counter for support.

"How can this….How are you….But you're dead!" she finally spluttered out.

"A very clever trick, don't you agree?" Tristan asked, dishing something from a pan on the stove.

She looked at the butcher block to her left and pulled a knife from it.

Tristan turned and frowned at her, but she didn't see any worry in his face. Was it because no matter how hard she tried, she couldn't keep her hand from trembling?

"And what exactly do you intend to do with that?" he asked, taking a step towards her.

Sydney didn't answer, because the truth was she didn't really know. Did she really think she was capable of killing someone?

He took the knife from her and she let him, feeling defeated.

"But why?" she asked as he set the knife on the counter, still within her reach. He was flaunting the fact that he didn't really see her as a threat. "Why would you fake your death?"

"When I realized Aleksandr's wife was working with the authorities," he said, turning back to the stove, "I knew it was only a matter of time before they connected the dots." He carried the dish to the dining table where a fork and napkin were already laid out, and Sydney followed. "It was obvious the moment I met Clara that she didn't believe for one minute her husband was buying art from my gallery."

"Unlike me," Sydney said.

"Oh, Love, don't be so hard on yourself. You played your part beautifully."

He started to reach for her cheek, but she took a step back.

"Don't touch me."

"Very well," he said, giving her space. "Can't say I expected to come back to open arms. Now come try this paella I've made for you. It's a recipe I picked up in Portugal last month."

"Why are you here?" she asked. "Why come back now if everyone thinks you're dead?"

"That is a question for another time," he said, lifting his jacket from the back of a chair. "And I took the liberty of exterminating your condo." Tristan gestured to a pile of small circular objects on the table.

"You what?" she asked, staring at them with a frown.

"Bugs, Love, they're bugs. Audio surveillance."

"You bugged my home?"

He laughed. "Oh no, dear, not me. But you're welcome."

Tristan walked out the door and Sydney dropped into one of the dining chairs, wondering if this was all really happening. The man she'd thought dead for the past six months had just shown up in her condo looking very much alive. And who bugged her? How long had they been listening?

Sydney spent several minutes in the chair trying to

process it all, debating if she should call the cops. Surely someone needed to know that Tristan Brandt was alive and here in Seattle.

She looked down at the plate Tristan had made for her. There was no way in hell she was eating anything that man had prepared, so she picked it up and went into the kitchen.

She was scraping it into the food waste when there was a knock at the door and she froze. Had he returned already? Was she going to know the real reason he had come back from the dead?

Shaking, Sydney grabbed the knife from the counter as she headed for the door. Maybe she could summon the courage this time. Looking through the peep hole, she was relieved to see Gavin, not Tristan, on the other side.

She swung open the door and saw Gavin's eyes immediately go to the hand that was still clutching the knife.

"What's going on?" he asked.

"He was here, Gavin! He was in my kitchen!"

He frowned. "Who was here?"

"Tristan! He's not dead!"

"Where is he?" Gavin asked, pushing past her.

"He's gone. He just left almost five minutes ago."

Gavin spun around and looked her in the eyes. "And you're sure it was him?"

"What kind of stupid question is that? Of course I'm sure!"

He tore off down the hall towards the elevator but returned shortly, talking on his cell phone, and Sydney could hear him giving her address. She assumed he was calling the police.

"Subject was last seen leaving about five minutes ago. I need all cameras in the vicinity to try and determine his possible route."

Why would Gavin be giving the police orders?

She set the knife on the table and saw the devices already sitting there. She turned to Gavin, who was still shouting orders into the phone.

"It was you," she said.

Gavin stopped talking mid-sentence and looked at her.

"You bugged my place."

The guilt on his face was all the confirmation she needed.

"Just get someone here as soon as you can," he said

into the phone and hung up.

"I trusted you," she said, her face going sour. "I invited you into my home, my *bedroom*."

"Sydney," he whispered, taking a step towards her, and she threw up a hand to keep him from getting any closer.

"I never meant for this to happen," he said.

"Bullshit! This is exactly what you wanted to happen. You knew he was still alive, didn't you?"

"We weren't sure. But we had reason to believe he might be."

"And you knew he'd come to me?" she asked.

"No. I was just sent in to find out what you knew."

"And what exactly did you learn by sleeping with me?"

"I'll tell you what I learned." He moved another step closer, and again she put her hand up, but he just took it and held it against his chest. "I learned I was falling for you."

Sydney wrenched her hand from his grip.

"Fuck. You. I'm done with everyone lying to me. Get out of my house."

"There's a team on their way to process the place."

"I don't care. Get out."

Gavin's eyes searched hers, as though he were hoping she would change her mind.

"Just go," she whispered.

He finally nodded and walked out the door. She went back into her bedroom knowing he was probably just out in the hall waiting for whatever team to show. She didn't care, so long as she never had to see his face again.

***

Respecting Sydney's desire for him to stay away, Gavin remained in the hall while three team members processed the scene. He doubted they would find much, but he could hope. Gavin kept checking his phone, hoping the crew back at the agency was having luck with any nearby cameras, but so far no word.

Brent Riker stepped out and Gavin caught a glimpse of Sydney on the other side, but she quickly turned her back to him.

"Anything?" Gavin asked Riker, who shook his head.

"Just a couple fingerprints," he said, "but that doesn't tell us where he is or what he's planning. John's finishing up with her statement and then we're heading back in."

"Do you have someone coming in to stand guard?"

Riker shook his head again. "I offered, but she's refusing."

"I don't care if she's refusing!" Gavin said. "He's already broken in once, what's to stop him from doing it again?"

"And he didn't hurt her," Riker said in a calming voice that only made Gavin more irritated. "In fact, she's says he was cooking her dinner when she walked in. He may be a wanted man, but I don't think he's a threat to her. We have no reason to force a security detail on her."

Gavin ran a hand through his hair. It didn't feel right leaving her here unprotected.

"Go home," Riker said. "There's nothing more to be done here. We'll watch the area in case he does come back, but my guess is he's too smart for that. He has to know that she was going to call someone. All that's left now is to figure out what his plan is. And that may mean waiting for his next move."

"Fine." But Gavin didn't feel fine about any of it. Problem was, Riker was right—waiting was the only thing they could do right now.

***

Gavin walked into his kitchen and slammed the keys on the counter. He'd just gotten the call that with all the people caught on footage in and around Sydney's building, not a single one of them could positively be identified as Brandt.

He pulled a beer from the fridge, popped the top, and guzzled half the bottle before taking a breath. Today had been nothing but a series of disappointments.

Knowing it was only going to lead to more disappointment, Gavin slipped the phone from his pocket and dialed Sydney as he leaned against the counter. It didn't surprise him in the least when it went to voicemail after only one ring. He didn't bother leaving a message and set the phone down. Seconds later it buzzed with an incoming text.

Please don't call me.

I just want to talk to you, he texted back. *Please.*

I have nothing to say to you, she wrote back. Gavin saw that as a good sign that she took the time to reply.

I know. Meet me and let me explain. You don't have to say anything. The message was marked as read. He saw the little dots signaling she was typing, and then they disappeared. Gavin waited, but there was nothing else.

He finished off the beer, brushed his teeth, and crawled into bed.

***

Sydney hit backspace on the words suggesting Gavin come over. What could he possibly say that could take away the betrayal and mistrust she was feeling?

He had said that he was falling for her, but that couldn't have possibly been true. How many times had Tristan told her she was the love of his life when all she'd really been was a cover for him? But what purpose could Gavin's lie have served?

Sydney tossed the phone on the other side of the bed and started beating her pillow before lying on it. She was so confused.

***

The next morning Gavin sat in one of the agency's vacant conference rooms. With a tablet in hand, he swiped document after document up onto the smart screen in front of him, hoping something would stand out, something that might tell him why Brandt was in town. He had gone through all the trouble of making everyone, including Sydney, believe he was dead. Why not stay dead?

Since Brandt had done so well staying off anyone's radar, there wasn't a whole lot of intel on him, and his dossier consisted of past articles found, none suggesting he was involved in anything illegal. One of the articles was a puff piece on a gala at his art gallery and included a picture of Brandt and Sydney. Gavin hated to admit it, but they both looked genuinely in love. She was wearing the same smile he had seen on her face at the Icon. Right up until she got the call about the break-in attempt.

He frowned, suddenly finding it odd that the bank's only robbery attempt had been just days before Brandt appeared in Sydney's kitchen. Gavin logged into the Seattle Police Department's system and pulled up the case file.

Very little evidence had been recovered. Apparently the would-be thieves had escaped when an alarm was tripped. The interesting thing was they had made it as far as the vault, and it was the alarm in the security deposit box section that had scared them away. And yet nothing had been stolen. Whoever broke in wasn't in it for money, they were after something specific, something stored in a security deposit box. And if trying to break in had failed, the next best thing would be using an inside person. Someone like Sydney who knew all the protocols.

***

Sydney stepped out of her office and found Gavin sitting in one of the lobby chairs. Pretending not to see him, she headed for the doors, but it didn't deter him.

"What are you doing here?" she asked.

"I knew you wouldn't answer my calls, so I had to come in person," he said, following her out onto the sidewalk. "You're in danger and I think you should let us assign you a security detail."

"I already told that Riker guy that if Tristan wanted to hurt me, he would have done it yesterday." She picked up her pace, but Gavin's long stride easily kept up. "I'm tired of you guys trampling over my life already."

"I think Tristan Brandt was behind the robbery attempt last week."

Sydney slowed down, remembering the familiar scent she thought she'd imagined.

"But why?" she asked, coming to a complete stop and facing Gavin.

"I don't know. There must be something in there that he wants. Did he have a box?"

"Yes, but I was able to claim all the contents after his death. He would know that."

"*Something* must still be in there," said Gavin. "And he's going to need you to get it."

Sydney racked her brain trying to think what it could possibly be or where it might be stored.

"Let me protect you," he said, placing a hand on her arm.

"Why, Gavin? Why do you care what happens to me?"

"Don't be so stupid. Of course I care what happens to you."

Her phone went off and Sydney jerked her arm away. "If you'll excuse me, I have to be somewhere."

She started walking away, and Gavin called after her.

"What about protection?" he asked.

"Leave me alone," she yelled over her shoulder. Sydney looked down at her phone to see it was only her mother sending a text. She typed a quick reply and continued the march back to her apartment.

*＊＊

Back in the conference room, Gavin continued to look through the same data over and over without feeling any closer to a lead. Riker was right; until Brandt made his next move, they had no idea where to even look for him.

"Have you been working on this all day?"

Gavin spun his chair around to find Director Rollins standing in the doorway.

"Pretty much," he said, turning back to the screen.

"Is there something wrong with your desk?" she asked, leaning against one of the other tables.

"It's quieter in here."

"Have you learned anything useful?"

"Maybe," he said, pulling up the police file for the break-in. "Last Friday, there was an attempt on the bank where Sydney works. A couple days later, Tristan Brandt approached her. I think there's something in the bank that he wants. And I think he's going to use her to get it."

Rollins moved closer to the smart screen and studied everything Gavin had put up.

"It's possible," she muttered.

"We need to get Sydney Holden into protective custody."

"Is she requesting it?"

"No, she's still refusing."

"Then so am I. We don't make it a policy of forcing people into custody. Especially when the perceived threat is based on a hunch."

"What about Clara Morozov?" he asked. "She requested protection and we refused. It almost got her killed."

"You and I both know that was different. We were in the middle of an operation and pulling her would have jeopardized it."

"Yeah, and that mission was a success," he said sarcastically.

Director Rollins' glare told him he was crossing a line.

"Until Holden changes her mind, we keep our distance. Keep working on what might be in that bank."

She made her way to the door, where she was blocked by Riker.

"Sydney Holden is on the phone," he said. "She's asking for protection."

Four

The broken glass made a clinking sound against the side of the garbage can as Sydney emptied the dust pan. She was making another pile when a knock at the door interrupted her. She panicked before realizing that whoever had made this mess of her apartment was not the knocking type.

She carefully stepped over strewn books and pillows to the door where Gavin and Brent Riker were waiting.

"There's a reason I called Mr. Riker and not you," she said as they stepped inside.

"What happened?" Gavin asked, ignoring her dig.

"I'd say it's pretty self-explanatory," she said. "It

was like this when I came home."

"Do you have any idea how they got in?" asked Riker.

"I'm not sure. The only window open was in the guest room. But there's no way to access it from outside."

"Is anything missing?" Gavin asked.

"It's kind of hard to tell in this mess," she said, waving a hand around. "As far as I can tell, no. Nothing obvious."

"Why don't you go pack a bag," said Riker, "and then Agent Maxwell will get you to a safehouse where another agent will be waiting."

"A safehouse? Can't you just post someone at my door?"

"We think it would be best if he didn't know your location," said Gavin.

"But what about my work? My life?"

"You should call to let them know you have to go out of town," Riker said.

"For how long?" she asked.

"We don't know," Gavin told her. "It could be a few days, maybe longer."

"Dammit," she cursed. "This is exactly what I was

trying to avoid."

"Take a look around you, Sydney," he said, sweeping his arm across the room. "Someone was looking for something. If they didn't find it, do you really think they're simply going to give up?"

She sighed, taking in the sorry state of her place. Every drawer had been emptied into scattered piles, pictures carelessly knocked onto the floor. She hated to admit it, but Gavin was right. This was no longer a safe place for her.

"Fine, I'll go pack."

She went into her bedroom, which had not been spared from the carnage, and carefully pulled items she would need from the mess. Obviously Tristan was behind this, but what could he possibly have been looking for? What did she have that he wanted so badly?

As she finished packing, Sydney called Jerry at the bank and told him she had a family emergency and that she wasn't sure how long she'd be gone.

"Call me if you need anything," she said before hanging up.

"Actually, you're going to have to leave your phone behind," said Gavin from the doorway.

"You're joking, right?"

"Afraid not. It would be too easy to track."

"Unbelievable," she muttered, placing it on the only bare space on her night stand.

"You almost ready?" he asked.

"I guess," she said, zipping up an overnight bag. "Not really sure what one packs when they go into hiding."

She picked up the bag and headed for the door, where Gavin put a hand on the sill to stop her.

"This is only temporary—we're going to catch him."

His face was only inches from hers, and he looked like he might try and kiss her. A small part wished he would. A very small part.

"Can we go now?" she asked.

He dropped his arm and they left.

***

The silence was killing Gavin as he and Sydney made the drive to North Bend, a small town just east of Seattle in the Cascade foothills. But every time he went to open his mouth to speak, he couldn't decide on the right words. What could he say? It's going to be okay? There's nothing to worry about? I miss you? The last thought was the only thing he could say with complete honesty, but he knew they weren't what she wanted to hear from him right now.

In the end it was Sydney who spoke first.

"Do you really think it was Tristan?" she asked.

He glanced at her in the passenger seat and could see the lines of worry etched in her forehead.

"Him or someone acting on his behalf," said Gavin. "I mean, who else could it be? It clearly wasn't a robbery."

"But why?" she asked, turning to face him. "What could he have possibly been looking for?"

"I don't know," Gavin said, shaking his head. "I was kind of hoping you could help me out with that."

She sighed and faced forward again. "You're the ones who did all the digging into his background."

"Not until after the fact. You're the one who lived with him."

"Thanks for the reminder," she said through gritted teeth.

"Sorry," he said. "It's just that—"

"No, it's fine. Even the Seattle Police thought I must have been involved. After his death they brought me in for questioning."

Gavin stared straight ahead, choosing not to comment.

"You knew that though, didn't you?" she asked.

He looked at her briefly but still said nothing.

"Of course you did," she said and turned to look out the passenger window.

Gavin was relieved when they pulled up to the small A-frame cabin nestled in the evergreens just outside of town. Agent Dawson stepped out as Gavin killed the engine.

"You made it," said Dawson.

Gavin nodded and pulled Sydney's bag from the back seat. She took it from him and marched into the cabin.

"You mind running to the store?" Dawson asked. "There's no food here."

"Sure," said Gavin. It might be a good idea to give Sydney some space.

"You're leaving already?" Sydney asked from the door as he started to climb back into the vehicle. Gavin could hear the fear in her voice.

"I'm just running to the store. Any special requests?"

"Oh. No, I'm fine with whatever." She started to

walk back in but then turned around. "Wait. Could you get something with chocolate?"

"Of course," Gavin said with a small smile.

***

It took Gavin over an hour to get back from the grocery store. Agent Dawson was seated near the wood stove, reading a magazine, when Gavin walked in with the bags.

"Where is she?" he asked, setting them down on what little counter space there was.

"She's been upstairs the whole time."

"Have you checked on her? Are you sure she's up there?"

"Relax," Dawson said, setting his magazine down. "I've called up a couple times, and I hear her walking around from time to time. This place is so small, I've heard her sneeze. Twice."

As if on cue, Gavin heard footsteps across the floor and the springs as Sydney climbed onto the only bed up there. He grabbed a Theo Sea Salt chocolate bar from one of the bags and went upstairs.

He found her sitting on the bed tucked against one end of the loft space with her chin resting on her knees pulled up to her chest. Her eyes followed him as he finished climbing the last few steps to walk over to the bed, where he sat on the foot of it, but she didn't say anything.

"I come bearing gifts," he said, placing the chocolate by her toes. The flats she had been wearing were on the floor and, once again, Gavin couldn't get over how sexy a barefoot Sydney was.

"Thanks," she said, unwrapping it. "How'd you know?"

"I saw a collection of them in your kitchen."

She broke off a piece and offered it to him.

"Thanks," he said, accepting it.

She broke off another piece and rewrapped the remainder of the bar before biting into it.

"Did you mean what you said?" she asked between nibbles.

"About what? About catching him?"

"No, I mean when you said what you had learned."

It took Gavin a second to realize what she was referring to.

"Yes, I did," he said.

"Why should I believe you?"

"Because it's the truth," he shrugged.

"As far as I'm concerned," she said, "you're just like him."

Gavin frowned and leaned back slightly. "Like who? Like Brandt? I'm nothing like him."

"You both lie about who you really are."

"Except that I do it to protect people."

"Funny, he said that's exactly what he was doing by lying to me."

"And I don't make it a habit of spending the night with people I don't have genuine feelings for."

"How do you know what you feel for me?" she asked, pounding a finger into the quilt. "How do you know you didn't just get caught up in the cover?"

Gavin scooted closer and took her hand

"Yes, Sydney, I did approach you with the sole purpose of finding out what you knew about Brandt possibly faking his death. But in all the times we've spent together, the only lie I ever told was what I did for a living. Everything else was the truth. It was the real me you were getting to know. I never intended to sleep with you that night, but I don't regret it. Even if I knew it was going to be the only time."

"What do you mean?"

"When we realized you knew even less about Brandt than we did, the operation was terminated. I was ordered to remove the bugs and stop seeing you."

"That's why you came over the day Tristan showed up."

He nodded. "I wanted to tell you in person. If it hadn't been for his return, that would have been the last time I ever saw you."

"And so when this is all over, what happens?"

"Well," he said, leaning across the bed, "chances are I will be asked not to see you again."

"And will you listen?" There was the faintest hint of a smile on her face.

"That depends."

"On what?" she asked. But Gavin had ignored her. It sounded like a car was coming up the drive, but a check of the time told him the first shift change was hours away.

***

"What's wrong?" she asked as he got up and carefully moved to the window at the opposite end of the room.

He put a finger to his lips and looked down on a car coming to a stop right behind the sedan, almost blocking it in completely. A man climbed out. Gavin recognized him from the agency but couldn't recall his name. And he couldn't be sure, but it looked like there was someone else in the passenger seat.

"Do me a favor," he whispered to Sydney, moving to the top of the stairs that were closer to back end of the house. "Put your shoes back on and climb out that window up onto the roof."

"You want me to what?" she whispered back.

"I need you to climb up onto the roof. I'll be behind you." Gavin knew it was an odd request and one that he would not normally ask of a civilian, but if there was one person he knew could manage, it was Sydney. He'd watched her scramble up rock walls enough times to know she was more than capable.

She did what he asked and Gavin listened from the top of the stairs as Dawson answered the door.

"What are you doing here?" he heard Dawson ask.

"Director Rollins needs you guys back at headquarters, so she sent me to replace you," the stranger replied. "Didn't you get the call?

Gavin didn't have a good feeling about this. He inched towards the window, preparing to hide with Sydney.

"What could possibly be so important it couldn't wait a few hours?" asked Dawson.

"I don't know. Why don't you call and ask her?"

"I will."

"I was really hoping you wouldn't say that," Gavin heard the stranger say just before a gunshot went off.

Footsteps could be heard running up the stairs just as Gavin slipped out the window and pulled himself up onto the apex of the A-frame, relieved to find Sydney straddling it.

"What are we doing up here?" she asked, shivering in the cool night air.

He pressed a finger, this time to her lips, and shook his head. Whoever it was had come up the stairs, and Gavin could hear their ragged breathing as they leaned out the window.

"Dammit!" they shouted. "They've jumped out the window! Search the area."

Soon after, Gavin heard the front door slam and footsteps come around the house. There had been someone in the car. They must have come into the house as soon as Dawson was shot.

"Stay low," Gavin whispered as quietly as he could.

"With any luck, they'll think we ran off into the woods. If they go far enough out, we'll jump down and drive off."

Sydney nodded as she pressed her chest against the roof.

"Grab the flashlights," someone shouted. A door opened, and then slammed shut. "You go that way, I'll search this side. Brandt is going to kill us if we don't get her back."

The two men split up, and with the flashlights, it was easier to know how far away they were.

"We're going to slide down, drop, and run to the cars," he told Sydney. "Got it?"

"How far a drop?" she asked.

"Not any further than I've seen you jump from a wall."

"But there's no mat to break my fall!"

"I'll go first and catch you," he told her. "It's not as far for me."

"Do I have any other options?"

"Stay here and wait for them to find you?"

"After you," she said.

Gavin tried to slide down as slowly as possible, but the steep cedar-shingled roof was covered in slick moss and he found himself moving quicker than intended. He hit the ground rather ungracefully, making more noise than he wanted to.

"Tanner!" someone shouted. "Was that you?"

"Now, Sydney!" Gavin called up to her. "Hurry!"

She slid down even faster, slamming into him, and they both fell.

"Tanner! At the house! I hear them."

Gavin and Sydney scrambled up and ran to the vehicles in the front. He checked quickly for keys to the car blocking him in but couldn't find any, so he pulled the sedan's keys from his pocket as they climbed in.

"How are we going to get out?" asked Sydney.

"Fasten your seatbelt," he said as he put the car in reverse and slammed into the other vehicle. With any luck, he caused enough damage to slow it down. Someone came around to the front of the house just as Gavin shifted into drive and hit the gas.

"Stay down!" he yelled as a gun was pointed in their direction. A bullet went through the front windshield and embedded into the back seat just as the bumper made contact with the assailant's knees. He fell across the hood and the gun was knocked from his hand.

A light could be seen coming around the other side of the house, and Gavin put the car back into reverse. Trying to make himself as small as possible for fear of more gunfire, he used the rear-view camera to maneuver the car between the trees and other vehicle. There was the unmistakable sound of metal against metal as they scraped past, and the driver's side mirror was ripped off by a nearby tree trunk, but they made it to the end of the driveway and Gavin tore off towards I-90, unsure if their attackers would be able to follow them.

"Are you all right?" he asked Sydney as she sat up, now that the danger of being shot had passed. For now.

"I'm not shot, if that's what you're asking."

He looked over to see her holding out her bare forearms.

"Unlike you, I didn't have long sleeves on," she said, turning on the passenger dome light to get a better look.

Her poor arms were red from scratches and splinters.

"I'm so sorry," he said, "I didn't think—"

"It's okay," she said. "Like you said, it was this or go with them. This will heal."

She didn't say anything else about it, but Gavin noticed that she was keeping them outstretched, not letting them touch anything. It had to hurt like hell.

"Where to now?" she asked as he turned onto 90 heading west back towards Seattle.

"Once I'm sure they're not following us, I'm taking the next exit and calling in to find out what the hell is going on. At least one of those men was an agent."

"An agent? But they're working for Tristan. I heard one of them mention Brandt."

"I know," said Gavin.

"You're telling me that he has someone working for him on the inside?"

"It would appear so. We've known there was a mole for some time now, but we assumed they had been working for Morozov."

She went quiet and Gavin exited the freeway. He parked in the back of the same grocery store lot he had shopped at less than an hour ago.

"I'm scared," she said. Her voice sounded so small, Gavin almost wasn't sure it had come from her.

He gave a small laugh and she looked at him, insulted.

"Now you're scared?" he asked incredulously. "As in you weren't before now?"

"Yes. Even when I called Riker, it was more out of anger than fear. I didn't imagine the lengths that Tristan would go to. Those men were shooting at us! And if he has someone on the inside, how do we know who to trust? How do we fight him?"

Gavin took her hand and squeezed it. "I don't have all the answers yet. But I do know that you can trust me. And together we're going to figure this out."

She stared into his eyes and nodded.

"I'm going to call Rollins and see what she says. I'll be right outside."

She nodded again and he started to climb out.

"How do you know you can trust her?" Sydney asked.

"I don't. But what she tells me will determine our next course of action."

Gavin stood in front of the car where Sydney could see him and dialed Rollins' direct line. Every agent had the number, but few ever called it.

"Rollins," she answered.

"Dawson's been shot," he said.

"What happened?"

"Two men showed up claiming you had requested us back at headquarters and they would be taking over."

"I did no such thing," she said.

"I figured as much when they shot Dawson."

"Is he okay?" asked Rollins.

"I don't know. Sydney and I fled without being able to check on him. If he hasn't called in…."

"I'll get a team there as soon as possible."

"It was an inside job," Gavin told her.

"What?"

"I only saw one of the men, but he was in fact an agent. I recognized him but I can't remember his name. Someone called out the name Tanner—not sure which was which."

"You're sure?" she asked.

"Yes Ma'am."

"But you and Miss Holden are safe?"

"For now," he said.

"If what you're telling me is true, then we can't know who to trust right now. Hell," she said, "for all we know this call is being intercepted."

"That is a possibility."

"In that case, you'll need to go dark. Keep Miss Holden safe until we can get to the bottom of this."

"On it," said Gavin.

"Goodbye Agent Maxwell. And good luck."

The line went dead.

***

Sydney watched Gavin put the phone in his pocket and walk back to the driver's side. He opened the door but didn't climb in.

"The good news," he said, popping the trunk, "is that we can trust Rollins."

"What's the bad news?" she asked.

"Her only advice was that we go dark."

Sydney looked at him sideways.

"That means going off the grid. Avoiding communication with pretty much anyone."

"Oh."

"How are your arms doing?" he asked.

"They still sting," she said, looking down at all the annoying little slivers. "Some tweezers would be really nice, though."

"Be right back," he said and walked back to the trunk.

He returned shortly carrying two small black bags, one of which he handed to Sydney.

"This should have everything you need."

She unzipped the first aid kit and found some tweezers while Gavin pulled a screwdriver from the other bag he had placed on the driver's seat.

"What are you doing?" she asked as he started prying the trim from under the dash.

"The car is GPS-enabled. I need to pull the battery."

It wasn't long before Gavin ripped open the interior, tore out a few pieces, and then tried to snap the trim back into place.

"Screw it," he said after multiple failed attempts and tossed it into the back seat. Then he threw the GPS battery along with his cell phone into some nearby bushes.

"That's it?" she asked as he started the engine. "We're 'dark' now?"

He gave a smile that helped to lighten the mood.

"Yes, we're officially dark. Now to find somewhere safe to hang out."

Five

Somewhere safe turned out to be a tiny little town off the beaten path that Sydney had never heard of. But it had a motel where they didn't ask too many question and were more than happy to take cash only.

"We'll have to figure out something else soon," Gavin said as they walked into the dingy room. "I only have enough cash for a couple days, and we can't use any credit cards."

Skirting around one of the two beds to the window, Sydney peeked through the curtains out into the deceptively quiet night.

"How will we know when it's safe?" she asked.

"I'm not sure."

She sighed. No one ever seemed to have any answers for her.

Across the street was a bar that appeared to be popular with truckers.

"Do you have enough cash to buy me dinner?" she asked.

Sydney felt Gavin at her side before she saw him out of the corner of her eye.

"You think that place serves food?" he asked.

"It says right there on the sign, kitchen open until ten. That gives us a half hour if we go right now.

She looked up and watched Gavin's forehead crease with worry.

"Is it really any more dangerous than sitting in this room? Do you honestly think we're going to be gunned down if we walk across the street?"

He looked down at her with raised eyebrows.

"For a woman was just shot at only hours ago, you seem pretty blasé about the whole thing."

She shrugged. "I eat when I'm stressed, and you forgot my chocolate at the cabin."

"Sorry," he laughed. "Wasn't really a priority as I was saving your ass."

Sydney laughed with him and it felt really good.

"C'mon," he said, closing up the curtains. "Let's go get you some food."

"And a drink," she said. "Wine also helps me relax."

He chuckled again. "Good luck getting a decent glass at that place."

As they walked across the street hand in hand, Sydney could almost pretend that they weren't on the run from her ex and his goons.

***

Upon entering the dark bar, Gavin did an immediate survey of all possible exit routes. He wasn't entirely sure this was a good idea, but he couldn't come up with a good argument why it wasn't either. And he and Sydney did need to eat.

She headed straight for the bar and asked for a menu.

"Order fast," the bartender said as he handed her one. "Kitchen closes in twenty-five minutes."

"It looks like your choices are fried food or…fried food," she said as he perused the menu over her shoulder.

"Were you expecting beef wellington?" he asked.

"I honestly don't care at this point." She called the bartender back over. "Can I just get the chicken strips and fries?"

"And an order of sliders," Gavin added.

"Do you have a wine list?" Sydney asked the bartender, who just raised an eyebrow at her.

"You're not supposed to be drawing attention to yourself," Gavin muttered as he turned to face the other patrons.

"Fine," she whispered back. "Scratch that. Can I just have a whiskey sour?"

"Any preference on whiskey?" the guy asked.

When Sydney didn't answer right away and he felt her leaning against the bar, Gavin was sure she was looking to see what was on the top shelf. Or looking to see if they had a top shelf.

"Don't forget we have a limited supply of funds," he said into her ear.

"The house is fine." She turned to him. "This going on the run thing sucks."

"Really? Because I always thought it would be a real treat."

Someone was leaving a booth in the corner that

Gavin thought had the best view of the entrance.

"I'm going to go sit down," he said, handing her some money. "You can pay for everything and order me a beer please."

"What kind?" she asked as he walked away.

"Unlike you, I don't care."

Gavin sat and did a mental assessment of each person in the room. Nothing out of the ordinary.

"I'm only teasing, by the way," she said, handing him the beer as she slid in across from him.

"I know." He took a sip of the beer. It was probably the cheapest one they had, and it was awful. But he couldn't give her the satisfaction. As he set the bottle down, Sydney was studying him, perhaps waiting for his reaction. He responded by taking another swig. He'd get used to it. And maybe he'd order next time.

"Now what?" she asked, giving up.

"We need to figure out what Brandt wants from you so badly," he said.

"I've tried, but I can't come up with anything. I don't have anything of his anymore. Surely he knows that."

"Maybe he doesn't. Maybe that's why he tossed your place."

Sydney frowned as she took a drink.

"But didn't you say you thought he needed something from the bank?" she asked.

It was true. Why try and break into the bank and then search her home?

"What if the bank wasn't him? Maybe it was just a coincidence," he said.

"I don't think so."

"Why not?"

"When I was at the bank that night," she explained, "I thought I smelled his cologne. It was so faint, I wasn't sure. But then when you told me your theory, I knew I hadn't imagined it."

"Could it have been someone else wearing his cologne?" Gavin asked.

"Doubtful," she said, crinkling her nose. "It was high-end stuff. I had heard of it, but Tristan was the only person I knew who wore it."

"So that puts us right back where we started. Wondering why attack both places."

"I wish I knew," she said.

"And you're sure he doesn't have another box at the bank?"

"I suppose it's possible he had one under another name. But then there would have been little to stop him from walking in and just emptying it himself. Or someone else with the same identity. We just have a name on file, you provide the photo ID and key."

"A key, huh?" Gavin scratched his chin. "Do you have a box?"

"I do."

"And where do you keep your key?" he asked.

"It's in one of those portable fire safes in my bedroom closet."

"Are you sure it wasn't taken today?"

"You saw the mess," she said. "It's going to take days to put everything back together and figure out what's missing." She took a sip of her drink just as the food arrived. "Besides, he'd still need me. "

"He needs you?" Gavin repeated. "Couldn't they just create fake identification?"

"At any other bank, perhaps, but everyone knows me there. It would be suspicious if someone walked in claiming to be me."

Gavin leaned in closer. Now he felt like they were getting somewhere.

"What's in that box, Sydney?"

"The usual," she said. "Important documents, a couple heirloom pieces of jewelry. Nothing to write home about."

"So nothing of Tristan's?"

"No," she said, shaking her head.

"You're sure he never asked you to keep something for him."

"He had his own box. Why would he?"

Sydney looked annoyed as she started munching on the chicken strips.

"He probably knew his box would be emptied and its contents either disposed of or taken into evidence," he said. "Think about every item currently in there. Are you sure none of them have a connection to him somehow?"

"I already told you…." She started to frown.

"What is it?" asked Gavin.

"I can't imagine it's what he's after, though…."

"Can't imagine he's after what?"

"A pendant necklace that belonged to my grandmother. I wore it for a function and he offered to take it in for a cleaning before I put it back in the box."

"Was that something you or he usually did?"

"No," she said. "I thought it was odd but decided it probably could use a cleaning after all those years. But what could my grandmother's necklace possibly offer Tristan?"

She had a point. Gavin sat back and pondered it. Brandt took the necklace out of her possession with the premise of getting it cleaned, but he must have had an ulterior motive. Then he remembered that Aleksandr Morozov had tracked his wife with a chip implanted in a bracelet. He wondered if Brandt and Morozov had the same jeweler.

"I don't think it's the necklace he wants," said Gavin, "but what's in it."

"In it? But there's nothing in it."

"There is now. I think he took it to someone to implant a chip or something. I saw it done to a Tiffany bracelet once."

"A chip?" she asked, dipping a fry into some ketchup. "What do you think's on it?"

"I don't know but it's obviously very important to Tristan."

"That's assuming the key really was taken," she said before popping the fry in her mouth.

Gavin sighed. Unfortunately there was no way to be sure. He couldn't call in and ask for help, and they sure as hell couldn't go back to the apartment.

"We need help," he said out loud. "And I think I might know someone I can call. Unfortunately it will have to wait until morning."

Sydney looked over her shoulder to where a small group of people were dancing to the music on the jukebox. It had been playing country music since they'd walked in, but someone had turned on an old 80's rock ballad.

"Dance with me," she said, turning back around to face him.

"Excuse me?" he said with a raised eyebrow.

"Come dance with me. What else are we going to do while we wait until morning?"

"How about get some rest? It's going to be an early morning."

"I'm going to dance first." She stood up. "And if you don't join me, I'll just be the crazy lady dancing by myself." She grabbed his hand and gave a gentle tug. "Please?"

Gavin fought the smile he felt coming on and slid out of the booth. "Since you said please…."

He let her lead him to the designated dance floor and realized that they were probably the youngest couple there, but no one else seemed to mind, and neither did Sydney. He wondered how badly she really wanted to dance, or if this was just her not having to deal with the events of the past couple days. Either way, he decided as he wrapped an arm around her waist and took her palm in his, it was great excuse to hold her close.

"Now is this so bad?" she asked.

He let the smile win. "No, I suppose not."

"Thank you."

"For what?" he asked.

"For looking out for me. For saving my ass back at the cabin."

"It's my job," he said, but regretted the words. It *was* his job. Yet it was also more than that.

"I know," she said with a smile and laid her head against his chest.

Gavin kissed the top of her head. "I hope you do."

They moved to the music for a little longer without talking until the song ended.

"We should really get going." he said.

She nodded and followed him out the door back to

the room.

***

Stripped down to his boxer briefs, Gavin leaned against the headboard with the sheet pulled to his hips. He flipped mindlessly through the TV's channels while Sydney finished up in the bathroom. He was contemplating checking on her when she finally walked out, wearing only her underwear and the camisole she'd been in all day. But without the bra. As she stood at her bed pulling the covers back, Gavin wanted to reach out and pull her into his bed. To find out if she still tasted as good as she did that first night. Instead he tried desperately to focus on the infomercial that had popped up on the television.

Sydney climbed under the covers and rolled over so that her back was facing him.

"Good night," she said.

"Night," he replied and switched off the TV before sinking down deeper beneath his own covers. He didn't really plan on getting much sleep that night, but he knew she would rest better if he wasn't pacing the room.

For the next hour, Gavin lay motionless in bed, his eyes studying the various shadows on the popcorn ceiling while listening for Sydney's deep breathing, and only hearing rustling as she tossed and turned.

"Are you asleep?" Her question sliced through the silence.

"No," he said.

More rustling, then Gavin's covers were being lifted and Sydney's warm body slid in next to his, her back still facing him. He rolled over to put an arm around her, placing his open palm across her stomach.

"Do you feel safer now?" he asked, nuzzling into her neck.

"Yes."

He loved how her cute little ass molded perfectly against him.

"You never answered my question earlier," she said.

"What question was that?"

"Will you listen if they tell you to never see me again?"

He sighed. This woman was giving him a hard-on that surely she was feeling by now, and she wanted to talk about their future. But he didn't mind. Who knew what the future held for them at this point?

"I don't know," he said. "The truth is, I don't ever

want to let you go. But it wouldn't do us much good if they locked me up."

She rolled over to face him with a horrified look he could just make out in the darkness. "Would they really lock you up if you refused to stop seeing me?"

He laughed. "No, it wouldn't be that extreme." He looked at her seriously now. "But it would likely cost me my career."

The frown remained on her face. "I don't want you to lose everything because of me."

"I told myself I would never be that person," he said, thinking of his friend and former colleague Reid Jackson, "to give up everything for someone. But now I'm wondering if maybe it can be worth it."

She still looked concerned, so he kissed her cheek. "But there's no point worrying about it now. We'll just have to wait and see what happens."

"I hate waiting," she said, rolling so that her back was to him again.

"I know." He kissed the back of her shoulder.

"What if they don't find him?"

"They will."

"But what if they don't?"

Pulling her tighter into him, he said, "I vow to keep you safe as long as he is out there."

"That might not be so bad, having you at my side all the time."

He swept the hair from her neck and softly kissed it. She turned onto her back and looked up at him.

"I guess if Tristan has to show up in my life again, at least he brought you into it as well," she said, and kissed him full on the mouth, pushing her tongue past his lips.

Gavin's chest swelled as he returned the kiss and rolled on top of her, planting a hand on either side of her head. Her lips were reluctant to let his go as he lifted his head and stared into her blue eyes, just as he had done many times before. On the end of his tongue were the words he knew couldn't go another moment without being spoken.

"I love you," he said. To his dismay, she frowned.

"I've never said that to anyone before," he told her. "Cover or no."

The frown disappeared from her face as she reached up to stroke his cheek, but still she said nothing.

"I understand your distrust," he said. "And I don't expect you to tell me anything you don't feel. I just needed you to know."

Fearing any rejection he might see in her expression, he pressed his mouth against hers and was relieved when she kissed him back.

As they moved in a slow, steady rhythm that night, their sweaty bodies melding into one, Gavin knew that this was what it was like to truly make love to someone. And it was the most amazing thing he had ever experienced.

Six

Once again, Gavin was slipping away from a softly-snoring Sydney, but at least this time he knew he'd be right back.

Many of the truckers that had been at the bar last night were now getting gas next door, and he was hoping at least one of them would let him borrow a phone.

The first person Gavin asked bought his lost cell phone story, and Gavin stepped out of ear-shot while remaining within a line of sight from the phone's owner.

"Jackson and Wells Security," answered a female voice on the other end.

"I need to speak with Aaron Wells," he said. "Or Reid if he's not available."

"Mr. Jackson is out of town, and I'm afraid Mr. Wells is with a client right now. May I take a message?"

"Could you just tell Mr. Wells that Maxwell needs a favor? Trust me, he'll want to take this."

"I don't think—" she started.

"Just humor me," Gavin said, cutting her off.

She sighed. "One moment please."

Fifteen seconds later Aaron's voice came on the line.

"Never thought I would see the day you needed a favor, Maxwell."

"Tells you how desperate I am," said Gavin.

"Obviously. What's going on?"

"Can't say too much on the line, but I'm trying to protect an asset and the agency has been compromised. Not too many people I can trust."

"Are you saying my name is at the top of that list?" asked Aaron. "I'm honored. Where you at?"

"A rural town in eastern Washington. But we're running low on cash and need a place to lay low. And perhaps some resources."

"Jackson is up there now. They just got back from their honeymoon and took a couple days to see family."

Aaron paused. "Let me give him a call and see if he has any ideas. Can I call you back at this number?"

"I borrowed the phone," said Gavin. "I can call back in an hour from another line."

"Sure thing. I'll make sure reception puts you straight through this time."

"One hour then. And thanks, Wells."

"No problem, man. Figure I owe you after the trouble I got you in."

Gavin ended the call and returned the phone. Now he just needed to kill an hour and hopefully Wells and Jackson could offer some help.

***

Loud trucks could be heard outside the room, and Sydney rubbed the sleep from her eyes, trying to remember where she was. When the prior day's events came back to mind, she looked over and found an empty half of the bed, causing her to sit up in panic. Had something happened to him? Then she heard a key turning in the lock and pulled the sheet tighter around her still-naked body.

When Gavin's face appeared from the other side of it, Sydney had never been so relieved to see him.

"Where did you go?" she asked.

He set a bag on the small round table near the window.

"Getting breakfast," he said, pulling out plastic-wrapped muffins and bottles of juice. "I wasn't sure what you would prefer, so I got a selection." He came over and sat on the bed next to her. "How'd you sleep?" he asked.

"Okay," she said, taking one of the muffins from him. "I kept having strange dreams. Not quite nightmares, but not exactly pleasant either."

"That's normal after what you went through yesterday."

"I was scared when I woke up and you weren't here."

"I'm sorry," he said and kissed her cheek. "I thought I could make it back before you woke up."

"Hard to sleep with all those rigs starting up their engines next door." She took a bite of muffin. It was sweeter than she was used to but not bad. "Why didn't you wait for me?" she asked when she had swallowed the first bite.

"Because I had a call that I needed to make."

"Is someone going to help us?"

"Possibly," he said. "I'm to call back," he looked at

his watch, "in forty-five minutes."

"And then what?"

"Then we see what they have to suggest."

"And you trust them?" she asked.

"With my life," he said.

***

A hot shower did wonders for Sydney, but the fresh feeling was short-lived after she stepped into the wrecked clothes from yesterday. She turned on the news and waited for Gavin to return, hopefully with a plan.

He wasn't gone long and walked into the room looking positive.

"We have more a comfortable place to lay low, and the best part of all is that it's free," he said.

"Really? That's great. Where?"

"My colleague's wife's aunt has a cabin just outside the Mount Rainier National Park. They're going to pick us up in Yakima and take us there. But we need to ditch the car. Even though it's not trackable by GPS, it's too noticeable with all the damage from last night, so I've found a truck headed that direction. He's leaving in ten minutes, with or without us. Are you ready?"

She looked around. It wasn't like she came in with

any possessions. "I guess so."

"All right then. Let's get going."

***

Gavin was a little uncomfortable with Sydney squished so close to the driver, a middle-aged farmer, but it would have been even more awkward with him sitting in the middle. Not that the driver had done anything, or even so much as looked sideways at Sydney. In fact, the drive was quiet and uneventful. It was just that Gavin found himself a little possessive of Sydney and didn't like the idea of another male being that intimate with her.

Two hours later, he was relieved when they were being dropped off at a popular farmer's stand just outside of Yakima.

"Thanks," he said to the driver before slamming the door. He put an arm around Sydney and they wandered the produce for the next half hour waiting for Reid and Jillian to arrive.

Gavin saw Reid drive up and he led Sydney to the car, where introductions were made once everyone was belted in.

"Sydney, this is Reid Jackson and his girlfriend, sorry, wife, Jillian."

Reid gave a nod through the rearview mirror, and Jillian turned around to shake Sydney's hand.

"So what's the situation?" Reid asked.

"Tristan Brandt is alive," Gavin told him. "And he's after Sydney. We think he hid something in her safety deposit box."

"What's your connection to Brandt?" Reid asked, looking at Sydney through the mirror again as he drove south.

"He was my boyfriend."

Jillian jerked her head back around. "Brandt was your boyfriend?"

"Yes," Sydney said with a frown. "Did you know him?"

"I met him briefly when I was abducted. He was waiting on the boat where they held me, but left shortly after. Something about taking his girlfriend to brunch. Wait, that wasn't *you*, was it?"

Sydney blushed. "Probably."

Gavin took her hand and gave it a squeeze. "Sydney had no idea what Brandt was up to. It was just as much a shock to her as it was to everyone else."

She didn't meet his eyes, choosing to look out the

window instead, but he felt her squeeze back.

"Wells mentioned Section Four has been compromised," said Reid.

"We suspected Brandt was after Sydney, so we took her to a safehouse. It wasn't long before another agent showed up unscheduled and took out Agent Dawson before pursuing us. Sydney and I managed to get away and call Rollins, whose only advice was to lay low until she could figure it out."

"Well, I never thought I'd see the day you'd call Wells or me for help," said Reid.

"That's what he said," Gavin grumbled.

"Do you have a plan?" asked Reid.

"Not yet. I just needed to get us somewhere safe while we wait for Rollins to get Brandt or we come up with something."

"Lucky we were in town then," said Jillian. "I noticed you didn't have any luggage."

Gavin and Sydney both shook their heads. "There wasn't time to grab anything," he said.

"I'm sure Sydney can fit into some of mine." Jillian looked at Gavin. "We'll see what we can come up with for you."

"I'm just grateful you guys are putting a roof over our heads," he said. "I'll live in these clothes if I have to."

"I might object to that," Sydney said, crinkling her nose. Gavin tried to pinch it, causing her to laugh as she turned away.

He caught the look from Reid through the mirror but pretended not to see it.

"Wells said he and Clara should be in later tonight if they can get a flight," Reid told him.

"I don't know if there's anything they can do to help," said Gavin.

Reid shrugged. "You never know."

***

The cabin they arrived at looked as though it had been standing for decades, but when Sydney walked inside, she was impressed by the interior. It had been recently remodeled, and while it still had the cozy cabin feel from the pine beams to the rock faced fireplace, it was well-decorated with current, comfortable furniture and all the amenities in the kitchen. This was a far cry from the cheap room they had left behind, and she couldn't imagine a better place to hide out in.

"Jillian and I will take the master bedroom here on

the main floor," said Reid. "There are two small bedrooms upstairs if you want to go pick one."

Sydney nodded and followed Gavin up the stairs. The two bedrooms were identical and directly across from each other.

"Would you prefer the sunrise or the sunset?" Gavin asked.

"Sunrise," she said and walked into the east-facing bedroom. But unlike Jillian and Reid, she had nothing to unpack. "Is there anything nearby where we can buy some things?" she asked.

"Not sure," Gavin said as he sat at the foot of the bed and Sydney sat next to him. It was only a double bed, not a true queen, but she didn't mind. "Jillian should know." He placed a hand on her leg. "Are you okay?" he asked, and she nodded.

They heard footsteps coming up the stairs and Gavin stood. Jillian walked in with a small pile of folded clothes in her arms.

"I brought a couple of basics for you," she said. "Some shirts and a pair of clean jeans. They might be a little short for you, though."

"It's fine," Sydney said. "You really didn't have

to."

"There's a washer and dryer here, and I've asked Clara to pick up a couple other things like a jacket, some underwear."

Sydney nodded. "Is there nothing close we can go to?"

"There's a gas station about a half mile away where you could get toiletries, but that's about it."

"Thank you," said Sydney.

"Thank you," Gavin echoed, and Jillian headed back downstairs. "So what do you say?" he asked. "You up for a walk?"

"I would love one."

***

The sun had long gone down when a vehicle pulled into the driveway. Reid peeked out the curtain to make sure that it was Aaron and then opened the door to greet him. Sydney watched from the corner as Aaron greeted him warmly, but when he shook hands with Gavin, the tension was obvious.

"Thanks for coming," Gavin said almost hesitantly. "You didn't really have to."

"I figure I owe you," said Aaron. "Not that I regret

any of the choices I made."

"What's done is done," said Gavin.

"That it is." Aaron turned to her and offered his hand. "And you must be Sydney Holden."

She shook it and nodded.

"This is Clara," he said, pointing to the woman who was pulling back the hood of her rain jacket, revealing shockingly bright red hair.

Sydney did a double-take and found herself at a loss for words.

"We've met before," Clara said with a friendly smile as she sidled up next to Aaron.

"At the gala," Sydney said, and Clara nodded.

"Tristan said you were the reason he went into hiding. He said you saw right through him."

Again Clara nodded. "I'd been around enough of his type to know. Especially when they were working with Aleksandr."

"So you were aware of what your husband was doing?"

"Not at first. After we were married he stopped hiding it from me, but by then it was too late."

"You must have thought I was so naive that night at

the gala," said Sydney.

"It wasn't your fault," Clara said, taking Sydney's hand. "You saw what he wanted you to see. This is on him, not you."

Sydney could see in Clara's face that there was so much more she wanted to talk about, but Gavin interrupted her.

"Now that you guys are here, we should probably head to bed," he said. "It's been a long day, and we could all use fresh eyes while we figure this out."

Everyone voiced their agreement, and Sydney let Gavin lead her towards the stairs.

"We'll talk more tomorrow," Clara said as they walked away.

Sydney and Gavin were almost out of sight when Aaron called out. "Aren't you sleeping on the couch, Maxwell?" There was no mistaking the sarcasm in his voice, but Gavin ignored him as they continued up the stairs.

"This really is what I think it is, isn't it?" Sydney heard Aaron say just before they were out of ear-shot.

***

"So what's the story with you and Aaron?" Sydney

asked as she snuggled up to Gavin.

"What do you mean?" he asked. "I told you, we used to work together."

"I'm not blind," she said, propping herself up on an elbow. "The tension between you two is obvious. And what was with his comments just now? Why did he ask if you were sleeping on the couch?"

"Aaron was the one tasked to take down Clara's husband. Actually, he volunteered for the job, and I was his supervisor. It was my first supervisory role. And my last. Thanks to Wells' antics, Director Rollins decided I wasn't quite ready." It was hard to keep the venom out of his words as he recalled that conversation.

"What happened?" she asked quietly.

"Clara offered to help Aaron, and along the way, Aaron apparently developed feelings for her which made things…messy." Gavin wasn't sure *messy* was the word Aaron would have used, but that's exactly what happened. He made a fucking mess of things. "When Aaron realized how much Clara's life was in danger just by being with Morozov, he wanted to pull her out."

"And then?" she asked as she laid her head on his chest. Gavin slid a hand beneath her shirt. He liked feeling her bare skin.

"I ordered him to send her back in. Or tell her to call the cops. But we couldn't get involved and risk the whole operation."

Sydney sat up and Gavin lost contact with her skin as his hand fell to the bed.

"I still stand by it. Morozov would still be out there and possibly madder than ever. And Clara knew it. When Aaron offered to go rogue for her, she insisted on returning to Morozov, knowing she was our best hope at taking him down."

"And it worked, didn't it? I mean obviously Clara isn't with Morozov anymore."

"Not exactly," Gavin said, and now he sat up. "A couple days later he ran off to Vegas, taking her with him, and when we still refused to get involved, Aaron called up Reid and the two took off to rescue her. In the end it was Clara who killed him in a struggle."

"Oh my god," Sydney whispered.

"Aaron still blames me for my lack of action and for almost getting Clara killed."

"Wow," she said, laying her head back on the pillow. Gavin did the same, facing her. "But what about the couch comment?" she asked.

"That would probably be because I've just done the same thing I gave him such crap for—getting involved with an asset. Letting it get personal."

"Well, I guess sometimes you just can't help how you feel," she said, touching his cheek.

"True," he said and kissed her. "So true."

***

When Sydney woke early the next morning and Gavin was still deep in slumber, she took that as a sign of how safe he felt in the company of Aaron and Reid. Or maybe he was really tired. Either way, she didn't want to wake him, so she grabbed some clothes and tiptoed to the bathroom downstairs. She could hear voices drifting from the kitchen as she stepped out and found Aaron and Clara shoulder to shoulder drinking coffee at the butcher block island. Feeling like an intruder on this intimate moment, she started to back away, but Clara looked up from the iPad they were perusing and caught sight of her.

"Good morning," she said with a bright smile, and Aaron raised his head as well.

"Morning," said Sydney. "I didn't mean to interrupt."

"Don't worry about it," Aaron said, getting off his barstool and heading to the coffee pot to refill his cup. "Would you like some?" he asked.

"No, thank you," she said.

"I was going to walk to the gas station store and grab some things," said Clara. "Would you like to join me?"

"I'd love to," said Sydney.

"Great. You'll let Gavin know where we are if he wakes up?" she said to Aaron, who nodded.

Clara led the way to the front door and grabbed her jacket while Sydney grabbed Gavin's. She inhaled his masculine scent as she pulled it on.

"I have an extra jacket if you would prefer something that fits better," said Clara.

"I'm fine for now," Sydney said. She liked the idea of wearing Gavin's stuff.

They stepped outside, and both women instinctively took deep breaths of the chilly mountain air.

"I use to camp here every summer as a kid," Sydney said as they started down the driveway and out to the street.

"Have you not been back since?" Clara asked.

"I came backpacking here once with some friends."

"You are way more adventurous than I am."

"Not much of a camper?" Sydney asked. Not that she could imagine someone as small and delicate as Clara in the woods. Although this woman did apparently kill her husband.

"No," Clara answered. "Never had much of an opportunity as a kid and certainly none as an adult."

"When did you…," Sydney hesitated asking the question on her mind.

"Yes?" Clara prompted. By her expression, Sydney thought Clara knew what she wanted to ask.

"When did you realize what kind of person Aleksandr was?"

"It was only months after we were married that I discovered what kind of monster he was," she said. "The first time that he…." She trailed off, and Sydney didn't need her to fill in the blanks. "I guess once he was sure of the hold he had over me, he stopped hiding what his family was. Especially once he became the head of it. Not that he ever divulged any of his secrets to me, but eventually there was no question what he was involved in."

"Do you think I would have eventually figured out who Tristan was?" Sydney asked.

"It's hard to say. With Aleksandr, his crimes were his life, his family. With Tristan, it was a double life. And he was clearly very good at keeping the two separate. No one had any clue who he was."

"But you did?"

"By chance," said Clara. "The day I met him at Aleksandr's restaurant was the first time I'd been back there in a long time. Had I not, I would have been just as naive as everyone else when I met you at the gallery."

Naive. Was that really what it was? Or had she simply been believing what she wanted to? But even now, looking back without the filter, she couldn't find clues to his secret endeavors. He had been the perfect, doting boyfriend. Always kept his promises, called her when he was away, and brought back extravagant gifts when he returned. Even her parents had adored him, and they got along so well. Yes, Clara was right. Tristan had been the master at leading double lives. She thought of his messages from overseas to say how much he missed and loved her. Who knew what he had really been doing all those times? Her stomach felt sick just thinking about it.

"Are you all right?" Clara asked.

"I will be," she said, nodding. "Just trying not to

feel like an idiot," she said.

"You know Jillian's story, don't you?"

Sydney shook her head.

"Doesn't surprise me," said Clara. "It's still hard for her. She told me the day I met her and hasn't spoken of him since."

"Spoken of who?" Sydney asked.

"Her father was working for Aleksandr. Selling him secrets and keeping an eye on Reid when he worked for the Agency."

Sydney's jaw dropped. "Her own father?"

"Yes, so if you feel like an idiot for not knowing that your boyfriend was an international criminal, imagine how she must feel." She stopped walking and took Sydney by the shoulders. "We have to remember that this is not on us. These were bad people, and if we were choosing to see the good in them, it's because we are good people, and there is nothing wrong with that." Sydney looked down into Clara's flashing green eyes. They were practically glowing. "So stop beating yourself up over it."

Clara may look fragile, but Sydney knew in that moment that this woman was a firecracker. It didn't surprise her anymore that she had defeated her monster.

***

Sydney walked back into the cabin with Clara to find Gavin sitting at the dining table with everyone else. Relief crossed his face when his eyes fell on her.

"Were you worried?" she asked.

"Not at all."

She raised an eyebrow.

"Maybe a little," he conceded. "Come have some breakfast. Jillian is almost as good a chef as you."

"I heard that," Jillian said, dishing up some scrambled eggs.

Sydney took the empty seat next to Gavin's chair. "It smells delicious," she said.

"Gavin here was just filling us in on your theory about the deposit box," said Aaron.

"Do you agree with it?" Sydney asked.

"It's plausible," he said.

"But how do we know for sure?" Reid asked.

"We need to know if my key was taken," said Sydney.

"But how?" Gavin asked her. "You can't go anywhere near your apartment."

"We could go look for it," said Jillian. "Clara and

I." She looked at Clara, who nodded her agreement.

"Excuse me?" said Aaron with a fork halfway to his mouth.

"Nobody's looking for us," said Clara. "We could go in, and if we can't find it, we have our answer."

All three guys looked at each other. It was obvious they didn't think it was a good idea.

"Oh, don't pull this macho crap," said Jillian. "You guys know Clara and I are perfectly capable."

Reid sighed. "She's right," he said.

Aaron looked less than thrilled but didn't argue. "Fine," he said. "But I'm driving you two into the city." Jillian glared at him. "Just in case. You two can watch each other's back in the building, and I'll be your eyes outside."

"It would be smart," said Gavin.

"But how will you get in?" Sydney asked. "I left my keys at the safehouse."

"Clara's got some skills," Aaron said, beaming with pride, and Clara blushed.

"So it's settled then," said Jillian. "When should we go?"

"How about now?" said Clara. "It's a two hour trip each way; this way, we could make it home in time for dinner."

Aaron stood. "I guess we're moving out."

Gavin retrieved a pad and pen from a bookcase nearby.

"You should sketch out your apartment and where the key should be," he said, handing the items to Sydney.

When she was finished, she wrote down her address and handed the paper to Clara, who was putting her coat back on.

"We should clean up first," said Jillian.

"Oh don't worry about it," said Sydney. "I can take care of it."

"Are you sure?" Jillian asked.

"Of course. It's the least I can do."

***

"I think this might be above and beyond the breakfast cleanup you agreed to," Reid said to Sydney, walking into the kitchen.

She blew a loose strand of hair out of her face as she paused her scrubbing of the sink. The kitchen had been spotless before she started, but now it was sparkling. But what else was she supposed to do with this nervous energy while waiting for the others to get back?

"I just wish we could call and check in," she told him.

"So do I. But we don't want to risk the call being traced." He pulled the lunch meat from the fridge and started making a sandwich. "Want one?" he asked. She shook her head. "If they don't make it back by nightfall, we'll turn the phone on and try calling them."

Sydney sighed and pulled off the yellow gloves. Maybe she would see if Gavin would go for a walk with her. She walked around the corner and came face to face with him.

"They're back," he said.

She, Gavin, and Reid walked out to the porch as the other three climbed out of the car.

"We couldn't find any key," said Jillian. "The entire box was missing."

"And you're sure you looked everywhere?" Gavin asked.

"Why do you think we took so long?" she answered.

Gavin turned to Sydney. "Looks like we were right."

"So what now?" she asked.

"We wait."

She groaned. "Have I mentioned how much I hate waiting?"

He could only shrug.

Seven

The rain pounded on the roof and it only added to Sydney's feeling of being trapped. They had been at the cabin for one week and were no closer to a resolution than the day they had arrived. She was feeling restless.

A car pulled up in the driveway, and she watched Gavin tense up for a second until a peek out the window told him it was only Aaron and Reid. They had left early in the morning to go into Seattle and see if they could learn anything through back-channel communications.

But the look on Aaron's face when he walked in the door told Sydney that they didn't.

"Sorry, man," Aaron said to Gavin, shaking his head.

"I figured as much," said Gavin.

"Can I have a word with you in the other room?" Aaron asked.

"Sure."

Sydney watched Gavin follow Aaron and Reid into the kitchen, closing the pocket door behind them. She gave a sigh and started shuffling the deck of cards on the coffee table.

"No news is good news, right?" Jillian asked from where she was curled up in a chair.

"Normally I would say yes," said Sydney. She knew Jillian was just trying to be positive, but Sydney's patience was wearing thin.

Raised voices could be heard coming from the kitchen, and Sydney cocked an ear, trying to hear what they were saying. It almost sounded like they were arguing.

"I thought you'd have a plan of action by now!"

Clara come down the stairs. "Was that Aaron?" she asked, and the other two nodded.

"I will!" Sydney heard Gavin reply. "I just need more time."

"You know what you need to do!"

"I told you no!" Gavin shouted as he stormed out of

the kitchen. "She's safe as long as she stays here!"

"What's going on?" Sydney asked, pushing herself up off the couch.

Aaron walked out of the kitchen with arms crossed while Reid remained in the kitchen, pinching the bridge of his nose.

"Wells here wants to use you as bait," said Gavin.

"What?" she asked, looking from Gavin to Aaron. "Why?"

"Brandt isn't going to make a move until he knows where you are. And we aren't going to catch him until he does."

"Is this true?" Sydney said to Gavin.

"What does it matter?" he asked.

"Is this true?" she repeated.

"Possibly. I don't know. Who the hell knows what Brandt is planning?"

"Then why couldn't we lay a trap for him? We know what he wants. We even have some manpower," she said, pointing to Aaron and to Reid, who was finally leaving the safety of the kitchen.

"No," he said,

"Why the hell not?" she asked.

"Because it's too risky. This whole thing has been about keeping you safe."

"No it's isn't."

Gavin's mouth went slack for a second. "What are you talking about? Of course it is."

"No, this is about taking down Tristan Brandt. The only reason you approached me in the first place was because you suspected he was alive. You were looking for him. And now you have the perfect opportunity."

"Fine, you're right. But I won't put you at risk to do it. We'll just have to find another way." He looked at Aaron and Reid. "And you guys are welcome to head home. I'll figure something out eventually." He headed for the stairs.

"Gavin…." Sydney called out.

"End of discussion!" he shouted, pounding up the steps.

Jillian headed towards the kitchen muttering something about lunch. Everyone followed except Sydney, who just stood there, staring at the top of the stairs. She had never seen Gavin so angry. She understood he was just trying to protect her, but what was the point of being protected if they had to stay in hiding?

She fell onto the couch and tried to resume her game of solitaire, but couldn't focus and soon found herself staring at the front window. Through the narrow gap in the fabric, she could see the rain continuing its downpour. Next to the window was Aaron's jacket, still wet from his fruitless excursion. She could make out the rectangular outline of his phone. It had been shut off before even arriving at the cabin and was only turned on outside the area. Just in case.

Sydney walked over to the window, listening to make sure everyone was preoccupied, and then slipped the phone out and into her own pocket. She pulled her shirt down to make sure it was covered and poked her head in the kitchen.

"I'm taking a bath. Does anyone need use the bathroom before I take it over?"

They all looked at each and shook their heads.

"I think we're good," said Reid.

"Take your time, sweetie," Clara told her.

Sydney forced a smile and then locked herself in before filling the tub. Now that she was in there, she was wishing she had thought to grab a sweater first. They all knew what needed to be done, even if Gavin refused to accept it.

She shut the water off and then quietly climbed out the small window above the toilet. By the time she made it the half mile to the nearest gas station, she was dripping wet.

Standing under the awning over the front entrance, Sydney powered up the phone. But as she waited, she wondered who she was going to call. How was she supposed to get a hold of him?

The phone picked up a signal, and she realized it was locked. Of course an ex-operative was going to password protect his phone. There was an emergency call option so she hit that instead. Not really sure where to start, she took a stab in the dark and dialed Tristan's old phone number.

It rang three times before someone picked up on the other end.

"Could this possibly be my lovely Sydney?"

"I know what you're after," said Sydney.

"Do you now?" asked Tristan.

"You need my grandmother's necklace from the box."

"Interesting. And why do you think I want the

necklace?"

"Because you put something in it when you took it in for cleaning," she said. "I don't know what, a chip or micro SD card maybe."

"I see. Well, let's say that I do want the necklace. What then? Are you going to give it to me?"

"Yes."

"Now why would you do that?" he asked.

"Because I'm tired of hiding. I give you what you want and you leave me alone."

"Mmm….Here's a better proposal—you give me what I want and you come with me."

"Come with you?" she scoffed. "Why would I do that?"

"Because you love me."

"Correction. I did love you. Until I found out what kind of a person you really were."

"That was all business, my dear," he said. "It doesn't change what we had. I still love you. Remember the life we shared. We could have that again and so much more. I'm offering you the world, Sydney."

"I have a hard time believing that a man willing to sell human girls for profit is capable of love. I was a fool for ever falling for your charade."

Tristan sighed. "Fine."

"I assume you've managed to ping my location by now."

"Yes," he chuckled, "I have."

"Then I guess I'll be seeing you soon."

"Yes, you will."

Sydney ended the call and started the short walk back to the cabin. The rain had lightened up, but she was too wet to really notice. A chill ran through her, and she wondered if it was from the cold, or from second-guessing her course of action.

***

Staring at the ceiling, Gavin laid on the bed, still stinging from the conversation downstairs. He still couldn't believe what Aaron had suggested. There's no way Aaron would have asked Clara to put herself in that position.

Maybe that was a bad example, he realized. After Gavin had ordered Aaron to send Clara back to her abusive husband for the sake of the operation, Aaron offered to run away with her but, like Sydney, she had offered to go back into the lion's den to do what needed to be done.

But this was different. He wasn't sure how, he just

knew that it was.

Gavin jumped off the bed. Now that he had calmed down, it was time to talk to Sydney and come up with a game plan that didn't involve putting her in harm's way.

Laughter was coming from the kitchen as he came down the stairs that halted as soon as he walked in.

"Have you seen Sydney?" he asked.

"She's taking a bath," said Clara.

Gavin walked around the corner to the bathroom door.

"Hey, Sydney," he said, knocking on it. "Can I come in and talk?"

No answer.

"Sydney?" he knocked harder.

"What's going on?" Jillian asked, coming around the corner.

"Where's a key for this?" he asked.

"Why?"

"Just get me a key!"

She rushed off, and he could hear her rummaging through a drawer.

"Sydney," he called out, "if you're in there, I need you to answer me!"

Jillian came back and handed him a small metal rod with a flat end, and he unlocked the door. The only thing on the other side of it was bathtub full of water and an open window.

Gavin turned to see everyone staring at him.

"She's gone," he told them.

"How?" he asked Reid.

"Through the window."

He rushed to the front door, grabbing a jacket as he swung it open.

He stepped out onto the porch just in time to see a drenched Sydney coming up the driveway.

She stopped when she saw him, looking like a deer caught in the headlights. Then her expression transformed into defiance and she started walking towards him again.

"Where were you?" he asked, approaching her. "Why did you sneak out?"

She answered by handing him a cell phone. Aaron's cell phone. Gavin felt all the blood draining from his face.

"What did you do?" he asked.

"We'd better come up with a plan," she said, "because Tristan will be here soon."

Eight

Gavin's face started to fill with color, and Sydney was nervous. She knew he wouldn't be happy about what she'd done, but….

"What the hell were you thinking?" he asked, grabbing her arm and pulling her towards the car.

Now she was scared. He stopped at the door and opened it but stood there, waiting for her to climb in.

"We have to go, *now*," he said.

"No," Sydney told him, summoning back the courage she had felt only moments ago. "I'm not running anymore."

"You have no idea what you're doing. Get in the car now!"

"I told you I'm not running!" she screamed at him. Anger was quickly replacing what little fear she had felt.

The screen door slammed, and she and Gavin looked up to see Aaron on the porch. Everyone else was peeking out the window or through the door.

"She called Brandt," Gavin said. "We need to get out of here."

Aaron folded his arms across his chest, not saying anything.

"No, Gavin, we don't," Sydney said, trying to even out her voice. "We need to figure out a plan of attack before he gets here."

Gavin gave a forced laugh. "You don't get it, do you? Brandt would never come personally. He's sending someone for you. He's not an idiot."

Sydney's jaw dropped.

"Didn't quite think that one through, did you?" he asked. "Now get in the car."

She closed her mouth. "I'm still not going anywhere."

"I won't let you do this!" he shouted at her. She would have been afraid of his volume if not for his voice cracking with what she thought to be concern.

"Why the hell not, Gavin? Why don't I get a say?"

"Because I won't lose you like I lost my sister, dammit!"

Sydney gasped, and Gavin held her face with both hands.

"I can't risk letting something happen to you. My sister thought she could do it too, and it only got her killed."

"I'm sorry," Sydney said, placing her hands over his. "I'm so sorry. But this is different. I have to do this."

Gavin let go of her face and slammed his hands on the top of the car, causing Sydney to jump. Aaron came running down the steps and a put a hand on Gavin's shoulder.

"Let's take this inside," he ordered.

Sydney had forgotten how drenched she was and welcomed the warmth of the cabin.

Clara appeared, wrapping a towel around Sydney's shoulders. She appreciated the gesture but wished everyone would stop babying her.

"Go upstairs," Aaron said to Gavin, "and let me talk to Sydney."

Gavin glared at him and then left without saying a

word or looking at Sydney.

Once he was out of sight, Aaron turned to Sydney.

"What exactly were you hoping to happen here?" he asked, folding his arms across his chest. "What's your game plan?"

She felt the confidence leave her completely now, and she avoided Aaron's eye.

"I—I don't know," she said. "I hadn't really thought that far."

"I see," he said, nodding slowly. "Then why did you call Brandt?"

"Because you said it yourself—we needed to make the first move. But Gavin made it clear he was never going to go for it."

"Then you should've come to me and we would've figured something out together. You didn't need to steal my phone."

Sydney knew he was right. All she had done was made a mess of things. And pissed off Gavin.

"Now what?" she asked Aaron.

"We proceed," he said. "It was a nice idea you had of laying a trap here for Brandt, but Gavin's right, he'll send someone to fetch you. Maybe we can catch him somewhere else, but that still means you have to go to him. Without any of us."

Now Sydney understood why Gavin had been so opposed to the idea.

"Reid," Aaron called out, "go upstairs and talk some sense into Maxwell. He needs to help us figure this out."

Reid nodded and headed up.

***

Gavin was attempting to cool off yet again, this time pacing near the foot of the bed. What could possibly have possessed Sydney to call Brandt?

There was creaking on the stairs and he turned, expecting to see Sydney, but found Reid instead.

"Did Wells send you to talk me off the ledge?" he asked.

"Yes, he did," said Reid, leaning against the dresser.

"There's nothing you can say that will change my mind."

"I understand that, but this is happening regardless. And we could sure use your help."

Gavin sat on the end of the bed and buried his face in his hands.

"Let me ask you something," said Reid. "When this is all said and done, when everyone is safe," Gavin gave a snort, "are you planning on leaving the agency?"

"Like you did?" Gavin said, unable to keep the disdain from his tone. "Hell no."

"Then every time you go out into the field, you're expecting Sydney to sit at home hoping for the best while you're risking your life."

Gavin slid his hands down enough to look up at Reid.

"That's assuming you're planning to be with Sydney after this," said Reid. "Maybe I'm wrong."

"No," Gavin sighed. "You're not wrong."

"I get why this bothers you. We all hate seeing our loved ones in harm's way. But this is her choice; no one is forcing her. And thanks to your temper, she made the rash decision to call Brandt. So instead of wasting time arguing about it, let's get downstairs and figure out how to take this bastard down so we can all get back to our lives."

Gavin dropped his hands completely. Reid was right. They all were. And he could sit back and hope for the best, or he could come up with the best plan to keep Sydney safe.

***

Ninety minutes later, everyone was packing up their stuff, leaving Sydney alone with Gavin at the dining table.

"Why didn't you tell me you had a sister?" she asked from her seat next to him.

"Because it wasn't important," he said without looking at her.

"Dammit, Gavin, why won't you open up to me? This is just like when you wouldn't tell me about your parents. Why didn't you mention her then?"

He sighed, continuing to stare at his hands on the table.

"Now's not really the time."

"Now is the perfect time," she said. What she didn't want to say out loud was that it may be the only opportunity.

"Please," she said, placing a hand on his back. "It's obviously important to you."

He finally turned in his chair to face her but kept his eyes on his hands as her took hers.

"She was a couple years older," he said. "We were never in the same home, but we managed to keep in touch. She wasn't as lucky as me and had a rough time of it.

Eventually found her way into drugs and petty crimes. But she was smart, God she was so smart. If she'd just managed to keep her nose out of trouble...." Sydney gave him a moment to continue. "A cop saw something in her and turned her into a confidential informant. Promised to help clean up her record if she would help them out. They went after a big gang. Sent my sister in with a wire in the hopes of taking out the top dog. It was discovered and she was killed for it. She was only nineteen."

Sydney didn't know what to say. She just wrapped her arms around him and he let her hold him. She understood it all now. It was no surprise he now spent his life putting away the worst of the worst. And why he didn't want her involved.

"I can't lose you, Sydney," he whispered into her ear.

"You won't," she said. "I promise you won't."

***

Sydney stood in the driveway kissing Gavin goodbye, trying not to cry. She was going to see him again. They had a plan. If only it didn't have so many damn variables. She only had herself to blame, though, for jumping the gun.

"Be safe," he said, thumbing her cheek.

"I will," she told him.

"I'm serious. If it looks bad and you see an opportunity to get away, you take it."

"He won't hurt me."

"You don't know that," said Gavin.

"He wanted me to go with him. Away with him."

His face hardened. "What?"

Sydney had told him in the hopes that he would feel better about her safety, but judging by his reaction, it had the opposite effect.

"Why didn't you tell me this earlier?" he asked.

"What does it matter? Obviously I told him I had no intention."

"Because he might try and kidnap you."

"Then I know you'll come find me."

Gavin pulled her against his chest, and she felt a sob catch in her throat. This wasn't goodbye.

"Maxwell," she heard Reid mutter.

Gavin released her and she looked up into his hazel eyes.

"I love you," she whispered, regretting all the times she hadn't said it before.

"I know," he said, touching his forehead to hers. "I love you too. Now go. Before I change my mind."

Sydney stepped back and gave him one last look before turning around and starting the walk back to the gas station. At least she had a warmer jacket this time.

As she walked out to the street, she could hear one of the engines behind her coming to life. With a little luck—okay, a lot of luck—she would see them again back in Seattle.

***

After only twenty minutes of waiting, a black SUV arrived at the gas station where Sydney was sitting on the curb, resisting the urge to go pee for the umpteenth time. A muscular man climbed out of the passenger seat and subtly adjusted his blazer so that she caught a glimpse of his holster.

"Miss Holden, I presume," he said.

She nodded and he opened the back door for her. She got up and prepared to climb in but was stopped by him.

"Could you put your arms out, please?"

She did as he asked and the man proceeded to pat her down. When he found nothing, he gave a nod and she climbed into the back seat while the escort got back into the passenger door. The driver was just as big and bald, wearing dark glasses. He said nothing as he got back on the road headed towards Seattle. Towards Tristan.

"Just sit back and relax, Miss Holden," said the first man. "We'll be there in no time."

Sydney knew that relaxing was the last thing she was capable of at the moment, so she chose to just sit back and weigh all her possible options.

***

Sydney couldn't believe it when they pulled up to the old art gallery. Tristan's old art gallery. It had a new name now, assumed by the current ownership, but still looked very much the same.

They pulled into one of the loading bays used for the bigger shipments, and the driver killed the engine as someone pulled the door down. Both men climbed out, and the driver opened her door. She stepped out and there was Tristan waiting for her at the top of the stoop into the back of the gallery.

"Is this where you've been this whole time?" she asked. "How did you get the new owners to agree to this?"

Tristan put an arm through hers, and she resisted the

urge to yank it away as he led her through the door and up the stairs to the apartment above.

"Here's the funny thing," he said. "I in fact bought it from myself."

"How?"

"Oh, it's not that difficult. When it went up for sale after my supposed death, I had an agent purchase it on my behalf."

"But why?" she asked. They walked into the small apartment upstairs that Tristan had kept furnished for late nights at the gallery, especially after popular events. Even Sydney had spent quite a few nights here.

"Oh, I have my reasons," he told her. "Some of them sentimental."

Sydney stopped short when she saw the dinner spread on the table, complete with candlelight.

"Remember all the romantic evenings we had when we were both too intoxicated to make the short trek home?"

"I'd rather not," she said.

"Don't be such a downer. Here, have a seat." He held a chair out for her, but she remained where she was.

"I'd rather just get this over with. The sooner I get you the necklace, the sooner you leave me alone. That's the deal, isn't it?"

"There's plenty of time for an early dinner," he said. "Now sit down and eat, Love."

Sydney swallowed hard as she sat in the chair. His last words were no doubt an order, not a request, and Sydney knew she had no choice but to entertain this man. Tristan dished up some food before sitting in the only other chair at the small oval table.

"I'm not hungry," she told him. Tristan was acting as though he had never faked his death to escape authorities, had not sent gunned men after her only a week ago, and it was unsettling.

"Nonsense. I've prepared your favorite," he said as he speared a scallop and smiled. "*Bon Appetit*."

"What's on the chip, Tristan?"

"The foundation of my empire."

"What does that mean?" she asked.

"Why the curiosity? Thinking of joining me, Love?"

"Not a chance in hell."

The humor left his face. "I do wish you would reconsider."

"And what happens," she swallowed hard, "when I

don't?"

"Eat, Sydney."

She managed to force a couple bites down but mostly played with the food on her plate.

"The world knows you're alive. You realize that, don't you?"

Tristan finished chewing before responding.

"Of course. I had hoped to remain dead for a bit longer. But I've always been adaptable. That's how I've stayed alive for so long. Not to mention out of custody," he said, giving her a smirk. "I know what you're planning, my dear."

"What is it you think I'm planning?" she asked, feigning indifference.

"Do you really expect me to believe you're going to give me what I want and walk away?" he laughed.

His words rattled her. Was she the one who had walked into a trap?

"What other option do either of us have? I want you out of my life forever," she said, "and apparently you need your empire back from me. We'll have to work together to get what we both want."

"You think you're such a clever, clever girl, don't

you? You spend a week in hiding under the safety of a trained agent and suddenly you're calling me to offer everything I want." He paused and then said, "Well, almost everything." He leaned across the table on one elbow. "Tell me, Sydney, does your protector whisper sweet lies into your ear beneath the covers as well as I do?"

She picked up her wine glass, wanting to throw it in his face, but settled for polishing it off. She could use the liquid courage right about now.

"Where is Agent Maxwell anyway?" he asked.

"I have no idea," she said.

"Hmm…," he said and leaned back to take a sip of wine. "I have a feeling we'll find out soon enough."

Sydney tried to control the shaking in her hand as she refilled her glass. She could feel the flimsy foundation of their plan giving out.

"You're a smart man," she said, setting the bottle back down. "I'm sure you'll figure a way out if we do."

There was a knock at the door.

"It appears our time is up," Tristan said, scooting his chair back.

Sydney watched him walk to the door and open it. She never expected the familiar face to walk through it.

Nine

Brent Riker stepped into the room.

"You're the mole," she gasped.

"It's time," he said to Tristan, ignoring her.

"Now, Love," said Tristan with an amused smile, "is the part where you hold up your end of the deal."

Sydney stood and Riker escorted her out to the street while Tristan remained in the apartment upstairs.

There was a light rain falling from the skies, and Riker handed her a golf umbrella he had grabbed on the way out. She opened it and he grabbed her arm.

"Don't try anything stupid," he said, pulling her close to him.

"What has he promised you?" she asked. "Money?

Power?"

"I don't see how that's any concern of yours."

"Just curious what entices a man to jump ship for the bad guy? Or have you always been a rat?"

The corner of his mouth turned up ever so slightly before quickly reverting back into a sneer. "I wouldn't expect you to understand what it's like to be passed over for assignments again and again. To watch agents younger than you, with less experience and brains, be sent out into the field over you."

"Seriously?" she asked. "This is all because mommy didn't like you as much as the other kids?"

"Speaking of the other kids," he said, jaw clenched, "where's your hero, Agent Maxwell?"

"Like I told Tristan, I have no idea."

Riker snorted.

It didn't take them long to walk the three blocks to the bank. Sydney shook out the umbrella under the awning while scanning her surroundings for a familiar face, but none were to be found. She tried to convince herself that was a good thing—they were remaining hidden.

"After you," Riker said, holding the door open for her.

They walked in and approached a counter. Recognition immediately crossed the face of the girl behind it.

"Sydney, you're back!"

"Hi, Ellie," Sydney replied. "Not quite. I need to access my deposit box."

"Sure," said Ellie. She looked at Riker and back to Sydney, who offered no introductions or explanations. The less, the better.

Sydney signed in and then the three of them walked back to the boxes. As Ellie pulled out the bank key, Sydney realized she didn't have her own key. But before she could say something, Riker slipped it out of his pocket and handed it to her. Ellie looked at them with confusion, but again Sydney ignored her. They both inserted the keys, and Ellie left them to open the box in private.

Sydney retrieved the necklace and started to hand it over, but pulled back.

"Don't play games with me, Sydney," Riker warned.

"I still want the necklace," she said, trying to find a removable part. "Tristan only needs whatever he planted on it."

Riker yanked it from her hands. "Consider it collateral damage. Now put the box away and let's go."

"You have what you want. I'm not going anywhere else with you."

"Oh, yes you are," he said, flashing his gun.

"Nice try," she said. "But you won't make a scene in here. And the second you pull your gun out, the guards will be on you."

"You forget that I'm a federal agent. All I have to do is flash my badge and no one's going to question me walking you out in handcuffs."

Sydney felt defeated. The plan had been for her to remain at the bank, out of harm's way, and contact Gavin when she had handed off the necklace. But Riker's stupid badge put him in a better position.

Reluctantly she put the box away, signed out at Ellie's counter, and walked out of the bank with him. She looked around again for help, but there was none. Panic started to set in as they climbed into an SUV that pulled up in front of them.

***

"She's in the vehicle," Gavin said, lowering the binoculars. "Follow it."

Aaron pulled the rental car into traffic while Gavin dialed Reid.

"Sydney's still with them," said Gavin. "Aaron and I are following her now."

"What happened?" Reid asked.

"Riker was with her."

"You mean Brent Riker? Are you saying he's working with Brandt?"

"Must be," said Gavin. "As an agent he wouldn't have been as afraid to make a scene."

"Dammit," said Reid. "Where are you guys at now?"

"We're getting onto I-5 south. No idea where they could be headed, though."

"I won't be far behind you. Call me when you know more."

"Will do." Gavin hung up.

"Are you going to call Rollins and let her know about Riker?"

Gavin debated. He should. She might even be able to help. But what if it all blew up and Sydney got hurt in the process? This was exactly what he'd been afraid of.

"Not yet," he said. "Let's see what happens first."

***

"This wasn't the deal," she said to Tristan as they drove off. "You have what you needed, now let me go."

"Because I'm such an honest man who always keeps my word," he said with a smug smile as he laid an arm across the back of the seat.

How could she have been such an idiot?

"Then what now? Are you going to kill me?"

"I'd rather not," he said, caressing her cheek, and she flinched, "but sometimes I have to do things I'd rather not do."

"What could I possibly offer you?" she asked, trying not to dwell on what his words implied.

"At the moment, insurance. Agent Maxwell will tread lightly so long as you are in my custody. He will be less likely to involve authorities for fear of risking your life. When I feel more secure, then perhaps we will discuss your release."

"When will that be?" she asked.

He shrugged. "Who knows? Weeks, months, maybe even years."

"And you plan to keep me captive that entire time?"

He cupped her chin, and this time she fought the

urge to react. "Let's put it this way, my Love—should you become more trouble than you're worth, I won't hesitate to do what is necessary."

Sydney pulled her face from his hand and stared out the window. They were passing Boeing Field now, Seattle quickly slipping away. She closed her eyes and fought back the tears. She had been a fool to think that Tristan wouldn't hurt her. Her life now rested in Gavin's hands, wherever he was.

***

The car pulled up in front of a building labeled King County International Airport, although Sydney had only ever known the airstrip as Boeing Field. Riker climbed out with a bunch of passports and papers in hand. The few minutes spent waiting for him to return were quiet and heavy.

"We're good to go," Riker said as he slid back into his seat. "The plane is fueled and waiting for us on the tarmac."

"No complications, I take it," said Tristan.

Riker shook his head and said, "I told you we could trust my guy."

The driver parked the car next to a similar SUV,

and two goons carrying small black bags jumped out, leaving only the driver inside, who drove off after the men exited.

"May I have the papers, please?" Tristan asked, holding out his left hand.

"Sure," Riker said, handing them to him.

Tristan opened the door and exited the vehicle before offering a hand to Sydney.

"Come, Love, it's time to go."

She took it with reluctance; what other choice did she have?

Tristan shut the door behind her, and as they stepped away, she heard a sharp noise in the vehicle and heard a thump against the tinted window where Riker was sitting.

"What was that?" she asked, frozen to the spot.

"Just tying up loose ends," he said with a pleasant smile.

She looked at the vehicle and then back to Tristan. "You shot Riker?"

"Really, I'm doing Section Four a favor as well. No one wants to keep a rat around. Now let's keep moving."

He tugged at her hand but she stood there, staring at

the monster before her.

"Sydney." There was no mistaking the warning in his voice.

She swallowed and let him lead her to the plane. Sydney felt the gentle touch of Tristan's hand as he guided her up the steps to the door. She shivered, and a single tear rolled down her cheek. Once the plane took off to god knows where, what hope did she have?

***

Gavin called Reid again. "They just took the exit for Boeing Field."

"That must be his escape route. Can't you call and have the plane delayed?"

"As long as he has Riker with him," said Gavin, "he has a free pass. I'm assuming Brandt already has fake papers made up for everyone."

"Even for Sydney?" Reid asked.

Gavin swallowed hard. "I would think so." Unless leaving Sydney alive wasn't the plan. "Just get here as soon as possible."

"Already on my way."

Ten

After waiting behind a driver that was too timid to make a right on red, Gavin was fuming by the time they pulled into the airfield's parking lot just as two black SUVs pulled out.

"Are we too late?" asked Aaron.

Gavin looked out at the runway and pointed to a plane just starting to taxi along it. "Do you think that's them?" he asked.

"Only one way to find out," Aaron said as he accelerated.

***

The cabin of the plane was small and plush, and it made Sydney feel that much more trapped. She was belted in a leather-trimmed seat opposite Tristan, gripping the armrests so tightly her knuckles were turning white. But it wasn't the impending takeoff she was terrified of.

The plane had just started to pick up speed when it began to slow down again and eventually came to a full stop.

"What's going on?" Tristan shouted over Sydney's shoulder to the pilot behind her.

"Some idiot just drove onto the runway, and now he's blocking my way."

Sydney could see the red rushing to Tristan's face as he quickly undid his seatbelt and strode past her to the front. She twisted in her seat to watch them. Could it be?

"Dammit," Tristan cursed. "Just go around him."

"I can't. I don't think you understand how this works." He started to reach for the radio. "I should call it in."

Tristan pulled his gun out. "You'll do no such thing," he said to the pilot, whose arm froze in mid-air. "Bring me the bag," Tristan barked to one of the men, who reacted immediately. Tristan dug through it while keeping the pistol on the pilot and pulled out a simple black phone. "Take this to him."

"What if he shoots me?" The muscle asked.

"Then shoot back!" Tristan yelled.

As the reluctant errand boy rushed passed Sydney, she unfastened her lap belt and moved to the front where she could see the familiar rental car parked in the plane's path, Aaron taking cover behind the driver-side door while keeping a gun pointed in their direction. Gavin, with his own gun and badge out, was moving to the side of the plane where the door was located.

"Sit back down, Sydney," Tristan growled. She couldn't but help notice he was using her proper name more and more.

"Why?" she asking, feeling daring. "Isn't this all a part of your plan? You yourself said we would no doubt be seeing him soon."

His nostrils flared and his face went even redder. She had never seen him so angry.

"Sit your bloody ass down before I shoot it."

She felt something hard pressed against her back and remembered the last member of their party, who clearly had a gun as well. He escorted her back to her seat while Tristan began dialing his phone.

***

The stairs and door opened up just as Gavin was approaching, and he paused. What if it could be this easy? But when the brawny man stepped out with a gun pointed at Gavin, he knew it had been too much to ask for.

"Where's Sydney?" Gavin shouted to him.

"I'm supposed to give you this," the man said, holding out something small and black. "A phone," he explained.

"Kick it over," Gavin said, not wanting to get too close to him.

The man did as Gavin instructed, and without taking his eyes or gun off the big fellow, he picked it up. It began ringing almost right away.

"I'm only going to ask this once," Tristan said from the other end as soon as Gavin answered it. "Get the fuck out of my way."

"Let Sydney off the plane, and we've got a deal," said Gavin.

Tristan's laugh was cold and grating. "You really expect me to believe you'll let me just fly off into the sunset as soon as I release her?"

"You think I'm lying to you the way you lied to Sydney about letting her go as soon as you had what you wanted?"

"Oh, I still intend to let her go," Tristan replied. "I just haven't decided where. Do I let her go when I land somewhere without any extradition laws? Or somewhere midair along the way? Alive or dead?"

"Do you really think fleeing the country is going to stop me from finding you?" Gavin asked. "Face it, Brandt, you've run out of options. Backup is on its way, and you know we're not letting this plane go anywhere."

"And what happens if our beloved Sydney gets hurt in the process?"

"Then there's absolutely nothing left to keep me from killing your sorry ass. But she's pretty tough—I think she can handle herself."

"So be it," said Tristan and he ended the call.

Gavin watched as the messenger stepped back into the plane and shut the door. He wasn't sure what the phone call had accomplished, but he hoped it didn't get Sydney killed. Time to come up with a plan of action, and fast.

***

Sydney heard Tristan's words as he hung up and wondered what that meant for her. His side of the conversation had not provided much comfort. She certainly hoped Gavin and Aaron had a better plan than just sitting out there and waiting Tristan out.

"Move," Tristan screamed at the pilot, dragging him by the collar.

"You can't—" the pilot started to protest from where he lay on the floor.

"I don't give a damn what you think I can't do," Tristan yelled back. "We're getting out of here."

Sydney watched in horror as Tristan began turning the plane, aiming for the larger, unobstructed runway, but they were going to have to taxi across the grassy median to get to it. There was a loud crunch and the plane bounced halfway through the turn. Sydney pressed her face against the window to see the winglet of the plane buried in the roof of the rental car.

Voices could be heard across the radio shouting to stop, but Tristan continued along his path.

"Shut up!" he yelled, shutting off the radio.

The pilot crawled into a seat and buckled up. Tristan's men did the same. It was going to be a bumpy ride. Sydney knew she was the only one left who could stop him.

Tristan turned onto the larger runway and began picking up speed. They didn't have long. She moved from her seat and stood in the doorway to the cockpit.

"What the hell are you doing, Tristan?" she asked, yelling to be heard over the engine noise. "Do you even know how to fly this thing?"

"Something else you never knew about me," he said. "Admittedly it's been a while, but I'm fairly confident the fundamentals remain the same. Now sit down before you hurt yourself!"

Instead Sydney took the only other action she could think of—she placed her hands on top of Tristan's, pulling as hard to the right as possible.

"Let go!" he screamed.

They were careening to the right and he fought to get it back on course, but Sydney was used to hauling her whole body weight up a rock face with these arms; he didn't stand a chance as the plane moved back onto the grassy median. Suddenly an arm was around her waist ripping her off of Tristan and she kicked out as she was being pulled back. She felt her foot make contact with something and realized it must have been the throttle, as the plane lunged forward even faster, sending Sydney and her attacker to the back of the plane. She could feel the plane lurching to the left again, Tristan was trying to get the plane back on the runway before it ran out. But the quick change in directions was too much for the aircraft and it rolled to the right, causing her and the other guy to go tumbling towards a seat. The nose of the plan ripped off and Sydney felt a rush of cold air just before blacking out.

***

"The car!" Aaron shouted after they had just ducked out of the path of the plane.

"Fuck the car," Gavin called out as he sprinted after plane. He had no idea what he was going to do if he caught up to it, he just knew he couldn't stand there and watch if fly away. His heart thundered and his legs pumped as fast as they could, but it wasn't enough. He was losing ground quickly as it sped faster and faster down the runway. Gavin slowed to a trot then stopped running altogether to watch in despair with hands on his knees, frantically trying to catch his breath. To his surprise, the plane started to veer right into the grass, then left again. And then his stomach dropped as the plane began rolling onto its right side. There was nothing Gavin could do but watch the plane rip into pieces before his very eyes.

Before he had a chance to react, Reid pulled up in the Range Rover and Gavin didn't even wait for the invite. He jumped into the back seat with Clara and they closed the small gap between them and the plane in seconds. When they stopped near the plane, he ignored Reid's warning about explosions as he jumped and ran for the biggest piece, the fuselage. None of it mattered until he found Sydney.

The right wing had broken off several feet behind, and the nose was buried in the dirt between it and the cabin and tail that still had the left wing attached. Of the two wheels, only one was still touching ground because of the single wing tilting everything to the left.

Gavin climbed through the hole left by the missing cockpit and immediately spotted three men, two of them unconscious in the seats they were still strapped to, and one tangled in the bottom of the seats on the right upper side. But no sign of Sydney or Brandt. One of the seated men wore a pilot's uniform, which meant Brandt must have been controlling the plane.

"Brandt's not here," Gavin shouted out to Reid. "I think he was in the nose of the plane."

Reid jogged off without saying anything, and Gavin

continued his search.

"Sydney," he said. What if he found her and what if….He shook his head. He couldn't go there right now.

"Sydney!" he called out again, this time louder, and this time there was a response. A muffled noise. It sounded like it was coming from the big fellow, the only one not seated. He walked up to him and checked for a pulse. It was there, but just barely. Then he saw a flash of blue that was the same material as the jacket she had been wearing the last time he saw her.

He pushed the other guy aside and could see Sydney pinned between him and wall of the plane. Her eyes weren't opening, but she was definitely moaning. She was alive! Gavin tried to pull her out, but there wasn't enough room with the big guy, in the way and he wasn't sure of the extent of her injuries.

Gavin was still struggling with untangling the other guy, wondering how he possibly got his body wedged into here, when the airport fire truck pulled up.

"In here!" he shouted to them. "We need help, please!"

Two men in protective gear climbed into the wreckage.

"Sir," said one of them, "we need you to exit the plane and get a safe distance from here."

"But she's stuck, I can't get her out! We have to get her out!"

The two men looked at each other, and Gavin knew they were going to ask him to leave again. "Please, just help me!"

Without a word, they came over and helped dislodge the big guy's foot and untangle his arms, and the two of them carefully carried him out to the ground.

"Don't move her yet," said the first fireman.

"Sydney," Gavin said softly. In the distance he could hear more sirens coming closer. Paramedics would be here soon.

"Sydney, honey," he said again and her eyes fluttered open.

She focused on him, and then a small smile appeared on her face.

"You found me," she said quietly.

"Of course I did. I promised, didn't I?"

Her smile faded, and Gavin asked what hurt.

"Everything," she said.

The two firemen reappeared, this time with a board

and an EMT.

"Wait outside, sir."

Gavin did as they said and found a spot to wait where he could keep an eye on Sydney the whole time.

Suddenly Sydney screamed, and Gavin started to jump back in, but Aaron, who had appeared out of nowhere, held him back.

"Let them do their job, man," he said.

"What hurts?" the EMT asked.

"My arm," she whimpered.

"That's a good sign if you have feeling in your arm," he said.

She was carefully brought out of the wreckage and strapped to the stretcher.

"Would you like to ride with her to the hospital?" the EMT asked as they wheeled her to the ambulance.

"Nothing could keep me from her side right now," he answered.

Eleven

When Sydney woke in the hospital, she wasn't the least bit surprised to see Gavin's head across her midsection, his hand still holding her left. He had stuck by her side the whole way here, and after pitching a fit, finally agreed to wait outside while they took her in for X-rays and CAT scans. She was lucky—aside from all the scrapes and bruises, the worst damage was a broken right arm. She was going to be released tomorrow.

She hadn't meant to wake him when she gave the hand wrapped around hers a squeeze but felt no guilt when his eyes sprang open.

"You're awake," he said. "Are you okay? Are you in pain? Should I call the nurse?"

"No," she whispered. "I'm fine."

Gavin scooted closer to her head and pushed a lock of hair back from her face. Sydney could only imagine how disheveled she must look and yet she didn't care right now. Because in Gavin's eyes, she could see tenderness, devotion, and love. Definitely love.

"Are you sure?" he asked. "You were pretty banged up."

"They've scanned me from head to toe. Twice, at your request."

"Wasn't really a request," he muttered.

"It takes more than a runaway plane to take me," she said.

He smiled. "Clearly."

"Did they find him?" she asked. "Have they found Tristan?"

"They called while you were getting X-rays. He had been thrown out of the plane and….He didn't make it. He's dead, Sydney."

She closed her eyes and took a deep breath. She wanted to believe it.

"I've heard those words before," she said, opening her eyes again.

"I know, but Aaron and Reid confirmed it on-site and I saw the pictures. I promise you, there's no doubt this time."

"What happens now?" She began searching his face. "What happens to us? Do you go back to work and I have to pretend not to know you or to have any knowledge of the Agency?"

She expected to see the tortured expression on his face, the same one she saw the day he admitted to not being who he said he was. Instead, a huge grin spread from ear to ear.

"I go back to work, but now that Brandt is gone, I don't have to keep my distance anymore. You just have to sign a gag order, and I can't talk to you about my job. Ever again." His smile faded. "Unless of course you don't want to see me ever again." The smile disappeared completely. "I can see how I might be a painful reminder of all this."

Sydney feigned a troubled expression. "I don't know if I could handle someone who goes running after planes for me. Or asks me to climb out windows just so I won't get shot."

"Yeah," said Gavin, frowning. "And I don't know if I'd want to be with someone willing to crash a plane to take out an international terrorist."

"Or someone who goes digging through dangerous wreckage to rescue me."

"Or someone who doesn't realize how much I love her."

Sydney smiled and pulled him closer with her free hand. "Oh, I'm pretty sure she knows it."

He grinned and leaned in even closer until she felt his warm breath against her mouth. "You think?"

"Yes, because I know she feels the same."

She closed what little gap was between them and with that kiss, she felt Gavin's promise to her and didn't doubt it one bit. He had already proven everything.

***

The first stop after leaving the hospital was at the Agency to sign all the paperwork Gavin had warned her about. It was tedious, but after working with banking security, she was used to it. As least they let Gavin sit in with her. He was busy getting started on his own paperwork at the end of the table.

Sydney kept stealing glances at him, excited that when this was all done, when they finally walked out of this building, they could be a normal couple. No more aliases, no more being on the run. Yes, there were going to be secrets with Gavin's career, but she knew it came with the territory; as long as there were no lies, no betrayals, she would learn to accept the secrets.

There was a knock at the door and a fierce looking woman poked her head.

"A word with you, Agent Maxwell," she said.

Gavin stood and joined her in the hall.

"Who's that?" Sydney asked the gentleman helping her with the paperwork.

"That's our boss," he said. "Now I need you to initial here, here…and here."

"That's Director Rollins, isn't it?"

He looked up but then looked back down without answering her.

"Right," she muttered. "Need to know."

A couple minutes later Gavin walked back in with the woman she was sure was Director Rollins. There was a file in her hand.

"Will you excuse us, Novak?" she said to the gentleman.

He nodded and left, and Director Rollins took his seat across from Sydney, setting the file down on the table.

Sydney could see her name on the tab.

"Is everything all right?" she asked, feeling nervous. She looked at Gavin for a clue, but he appeared relaxed. Pleased, even.

"My name is Laura Rollins," she said, extending a hand. "I'm the director here."

Sydney took it. "A pleasure to finally meet you." She saw a slight smile crack on the otherwise stern face.

"I would like to offer you a job, Miss Holden," said the director.

"A job? Here?"

Rollins gave a nod.

"As an agent?"

"Nothing such as that," Rollins said with a polite smile. "We would like to have you here in the office working with our security team."

"Really?"

"I've been looking into you." Rollins opened the file. "I'm impressed with the work you have done for Northwest Union Bank, and I think you could be an asset here."

Sydney couldn't believe what they were asking—it was such an honor. She looked at Gavin, who wasn't even trying to hide his excitement. They would be working together.

"So what do you say, Miss Holden, would you be interested in working for us?" Rollins asked. "You would have to maintain an even higher level of confidentiality than before. You won't be able to tell your friends and family who you really work for. On the record you would be working for Dauphine Security Systems. Could you handle that?"

"Absolutely," she said. "I do have a question though."

"What's that?"

"What exactly is the policy for dating coworkers?"

There was the crack of a smile again. "Since you two would not be working together, it would be allowed, though you will have to fill out a form with HR."

Sydney nodded. She was familiar with the practice.

"I can also say," and this time there was a twinkle in Rollins' eye, "there are slightly fewer secrets when both parties are working for the same black-ops organization."

"In that case, Director Rollins," Sydney held out her hand, "I would love to come work for you."

Acknowledgments

I want to say a very big thank you to my family for their support and understanding on this project. It's amazing how much I managed to accomplish in such a short amount of time, and they suffered through it all! I want to thank my editor Carrie for her ninja skills in the proofreading department. She is a pleasure to work with and I can't give her enough kudos. Thank you as always to Cattigan for being my beta reader extraordinaire. I know it's such a chore for you (wink wink), but someone's got to do it! And thank you to everyone who has taken the time to read what I have written, it means the world to me.

Don't miss these other titles by Alex Strong

Island Runaway

CrossFire: Love & Lies Book 1

No Way Out: Love & Lies Book 2

Available on-line at Amazon, Barnes & Noble, and many other e-book retailers.

Follow Alex on Facebook and Twitter to find out what she's working on next:

Facebook.com/alexstrongwrites

@TheAlex_Strong

About the Author

Alex Strong has loved stories, whether she's reading them or telling them, since she was very young. But it wasn't until after the birth of her youngest son that she realized how much she wanted to be an author. Her past lives include working as a waitress, a sales clerk, and a nanny. Though she has been all around the world, including two years living in the Philippines as a child, Alex is proud to call the Pacific Northwest her home, and lives in the Seattle suburbs with her husband, their two boys, and two fluffy dogs.